THE COUNTRY LAWYER

A Legal Thriller

THE
COUNTRY
LAWYER

A Legal Thriller

John W. Dennehy

Macabre Tales Publishing

The Country Lawyer © 2022 by John W. Dennehy

Macabre Tales Publishing
127 Main Street, Suite 1
Nashua, NH 03060

Written by John W. Dennehy
Cover Design by Carys C. Dennehy

First Printed in the United States of America, 2023.

CONTENTS

CHAPTER ONE

WADE GARRETT stood by a window in the old brick and mortar mill building. He watched the river outside cascade over the dam, as a couple of his business partners squabbled about the big promissory note coming due.

Orange, yellow, and red leaves whisked along the surface of the water in the downstream current. Autumn had crept up rather quickly. Soon, they would be in the dead of winter; new manufacturing orders would decline and their revenue along with it.

"How we going to get caught up?" asked Tyler Cummings.

"Never mind that," Scott Bancroft snapped. "Just how did we get into this mess to begin with? That's what I want to know."

Wade turned and faced them. Tyler glanced at the floor, avoiding him. Bancroft returned the stare. The rich kid was angry and wouldn't back down. This would take some smooth talking, at least for now.

"Orders are down, and we couldn't keep up with the little demand we had," Wade said. "Heck, we've got ships sitting off ports without people to unload materials."

"Why can't we get another government loan?" Tyler said.

Wade shook his head. "Because they're tapped out."

"You've overextended us," Bancroft yelled, pointing a finger at Wade.

"Look, we've got to deal with the situation. Find a way out of this," Wade said. "Arguing about how we got here isn't going to help any of us."

A lull fell over the discussion as they considered his words.

The three of them stood in a near empty supply room at the back corner of the building. The mill was located in Wilton, New Hampshire, along the Souhegan River. During the industrial revolution, the mill had been a manufacturing facility, powered by the river. Now, it was used for fabricating metal products for component parts found in industrial equipment.

"Can't we get Jenkins to give us more time?" asked Tyler.

"I've tried," Wade said. "He's coming by here tonight. We either pay enough to get caught up, or he's calling in the loan. The sheriff will have us out in a month."

"How about your father?" Tyler said to Bancroft.

"Can't do it. He's hurting like everyone else."

This was the reason Wade had called the meeting. He wanted to find out if there was a workable solution. Bancroft's father was a successful businessman in the area. They'd turned to him in the past.

"You sure?" Wade said.

"I'm certain." And Bancroft looked it.

Wind rattled the old windows, and a chill ran up Wade's spine. He pulled his denim trucker's jacket with a Sherpa lined collar tight, then worked a couple buttons through the holes. It was oil stained from working on the machinery, like his Wrangler jeans and work boots.

The other two were college boys. Bancroft oversaw sales and looked the part, with slicked-back dark hair. Tyler was meek and handled the bookkeeping, but he only managed accounts receivable and payable. Wade kept a tight leash on the business loans and their salaries.

"So, what can we do?" Bancroft said, looking glum.

"If Jenkins won't agree to a workable solution," Wade said, rubbing a hand over three days of stubble on his chin. "We'll have to torch the place."

CHAPTER TWO

WADE GARRETT sat behind a metal desk in the ramshackle office of the old mill building, while Tyler Cummings and Scott Bancroft stood along the walls, flanking their visitor. Herbert Jenkins sat on the other side of the desk in an old industrial chair, with metal framing and soft vinyl cushions.

The old man didn't look intimidated. He wasn't about to compromise his terms.

"We both know you boys have come into tough times," Jenkins said. "Heck, many small businesses across the country are folding, while others are flourishing. These are odd times. I can sympathize with you. But I need to know when I'm going to get paid."

Wade shrugged. "We're here trying to work things out."

"Sure, you are," Jenkins said. "I hear you talking. But I ain't seen any money in my pocket."

"This is a workable situation," Wade said. "We've paid back a lot of the loan. You can trust us to get through this. I promise, you'll get your money."

"When?" Jenkins eyeballed him.

"Can't say for certain. These are trying times, like you mentioned."

"I'm not going to pause your payments without a specific plan in place for you to get caught up," Jenkins said, crossing his arms.

"We can't commit to something specific right now."

"Then there's nothing to discuss."

"Look, if you call in the loan," Wade said. "You won't ever get paid."

"I'll get what you've paid to date. And I'll get the mill back."

The comment caught Wade off guard. So, that was the old man's angle.

"I know a dairy farmer over in Milford," Jenkins said. "Sold the same farm three times."

"Not sure you can get another buyer for the mill," Wade pled. "You'll be stuck with the property. There will be taxes, oil and electric bills."

Jenkins considered Wade's comment. Then, he looked over at Tyler for a moment. Tyler sheepishly glanced at the floor. Jenkins turned his head and studied Bancroft. Finally, the old man looked back at Wade. "If his father guarantees the plan," Jenkins said, motioning with a thumb at Bancroft. "Then, I expect we can work something out."

"No way!" Bancroft yelled.

"Why not?" Jenkins sounded truly interested to hear the explanation.

"My father has nothing to do with this," Bancroft said. "Besides, he's—"

"There's no need to fight about this," Wade said, interrupting.

"I'd like to hear what he's got to say," Jenkins said.

Wade knew exactly what Bancroft would say. He'd blabber that his father wasn't in a position to help. Couldn't help if he wanted to. But they needed time more than anything. People in debt always fight for time. Leaving Jenkins thinking Bancroft's father might provide security could at least buy them a couple weeks.

"There's no reason for us to argue," Wade said. "You've made a proposal. We should consider it."

"And what's my proposal?" asked Jenkins.

"You want a definitive plan to get caught up, and you want security."

Bancroft shook his head, dismayed. Fortunately, the old man didn't see it.

Jenkins smiled. "That about sums it up."

"We'll need some time to talk to the bank and Mr. Bancroft," Wade said. "Then we can get you a definitive proposal."

"You have one week," Jenkins said, standing up.

When the old man turned to leave, Wade scowled at Bancroft, signaling for the younger man to keep his mouth shut.

"Tyler can walk you out," Wade said.

"Much obliged," Jenkins replied.

As soon as Jenkins and Tyler were out of earshot, Wade let loose on Bancroft. "What the hell were you thinking?"

"Me?" Bancroft said. "You know my father can't help."

"This isn't about whether or not your father *can* help. Dumbass." Wade shook his head. "It's about buying us more time. We need to keep Jenkins thinking that we can come through, as long as possible."

"What's that going to do?" Bancroft said. "We're already in too deep."

"Tomorrow is always better than today when you're the debtor."

CHAPTER THREE

MASON WALTERS stood fly-fishing in the middle of a flowing river near an outcrop of smooth boulders. A deep pool of water lay on the far side of the rocks. The cases at his law office could wait a little longer.

He dropped a line slightly downstream and let his fly run with the current.

A late autumn breeze whipped into his cheeks, and the cold water, circling his waders, numbed his aging knees.

Then, a trout broke the surface, took the fly, and lunged back into the stream. A big fish. Mason tugged the line with his left hand, setting the hook. He yanked the rod back with his right, attempting to send the hook home. And then, he let the line go and watched it whip downstream, as the trout made its flight. The reel spun and zinged out the rhythm of the unwinding spool, a familiar cadence of a fly fisher dancing with a precious game fish.

Once the trout wore itself down, Mason began reeling it in, churning the reel-handle with his left hand, while holding the corky rod-handle in his right.

The effort lessened the longer he labored at retrieving the fish.

A powerful thrust suddenly pulled at the end of the line, yanking him and loosening his footing. Mason teetered on slippery stones in the riverbed and feared plunging into the frigid water. His agile six-foot frame swayed as he floundered in the current. Dangerous rocks and boulders were crowded along the riverbank, making a fall into the rushing water potentially perilous.

Mason let go of the line, letting the fish run with the hook, while he regained his balance. He waited a moment, then he reeled in the slack. When the line went taut, the big trout writhed on the end, and shot from the water, twisting in the morning sunlight.

It landed in the river with a splash and gave Mason another fight.

"Like a criminal on the run," Mason muttered.

He worked and labored, then got the fish within six feet of himself. Mason headed closer to shore before he reeled the trout all the way in. Cupping the fish's belly in one hand, he wriggled the hook loose with the other. A brownish fish with a bright orange belly, it was adorned with yellow and red spots.

Mason shook his head, amazed at the sight of the brook trout. *A magnificent creature*, he thought.

After removing the hook from the trout's lip, Mason reached into the front pouch of his waders and pulled out his cellphone. He took a photograph of the prize, with his rod set in the shallows beside it. Then, he lowered the trout into the water, and let its gills gather oxygen.

He released the fish and watched it rifle through the current then disappear downstream.

Freedom is a precious commodity, he thought.

CHAPTER FOUR

A WEEK LATER, the follow up meeting with Jenkins didn't go according to plan. Wade tried to focus on a payment schedule he'd devised, but the old man only wanted to know if there would be any security.

Jenkins had fixated on a guarantee from Bancroft's father until it drove Wade nuts.

"Enough!" Wade bellowed. "I've had enough with all this talk about security."

"Well, I need it if we're going to move forward," Jenkins said.

"You're not going to get it," Bancroft cut in.

"Then I guess we're through here," Jenkins said.

Grasping the arms of his chair, Jenkins pushed upward and stood. He paused before leaving as though waiting for Wade to come around. Everyone had their coats on due to the cold temperature in the building, so the old man was ready to depart on a moment's notice.

Tyler shook his head, dismayed. Then, the boy marched out of the room.

Wade sat back and eyeballed the old man. "Why don't you sit back down?"

The old man hesitated. "Afraid I don't like your tone," he said after a moment.

"We're not through talking," Wade said in a churlish timbre.

Jenkins turned away from Wade's penetrating stare. He perused the office.

Wade followed the old man's gaze, as the old-timer traced his eyes around the room. It was bereft of personal items. A standard factory office, it had a desk and a couple of chairs.

The walls in the office were knotty pine, aged to a warm yellow and orange. Several metal filing cabinets were situated against a wall, and a bookcase full of binders and notebooks leaned against another. The floor was made of thick planks, like those found on the upper factory floors. At one point, the wide planks were painted gray. Now, the old planks were almost bare. Most of the paint had chipped away, leaving dark, exposed wood.

"I like what you did with the place," Jenkins finally said.

"We haven't changed a thing since you left," Wade snapped.

"That's what I like about it." Jenkins grinned. "Makes moving back in a simple process."

"You've got some nerve," Bancroft said, bunching his fists.

Jenkins trundled towards the door. "You'll be hearing from my lawyers."

Wade considered the comment, as Jenkins headed out across the factory floor.

The old man used a law firm over in Peterborough. It was the only multi-lawyer firm in the area. They had about ten attorneys. The managing lawyer was a seasoned litigator. He'd grown up in the area and had gone to the Ivy League for college and law school. Now, the lawyer sported a long, flowing beard and bowtie. He looked like the guy on a PBS gardening program meets a Boson blue blood. Litigation would clean them out.

A harsh wind blew. It rattled the old factory windows. Cold air permeated the building, a harbinger of the days to come. Wade expected a frigid winter with financials pushing them right out into the cold. Glancing outside, he noticed snowflakes whisking in a hazy glow, cast from a nearby streetlamp.

A truck fired up. The headlights shot through the parking lot, then the vehicle whipped onto the country road and tore off into the darkness. It was too quick to have been Jenkins.

Maybe it was Tyler, Wade thought. *Or a worker leaving late.*

The office door slammed shut and stirred Wade from his thoughts.

A frosted glass window in the upper half of the wooden door

shook with the force of the door banging closed. Bancroft stood beside the door, and a primal rage consumed him.

"We need to do something about Jenkins, right now," he said.

***

WADE GARRETT fumbled around in the storage room, which was located on the basement level of the mill building. He busied himself returning tools to hooks, placing them on a pegboard and shoving them into toolboxes propped against an outside wall.

Working on machinery usually helped ease his mind. It required problem solving and served to block out whatever troubled him. After Jenkins walked out of the office, Wade had repaired equipment to take his mind off the situation. Thoughts of their predicament weren't so easy to squelch, however. He couldn't stop thinking about Jenkins. Wade wondered if he had kept his cool and not snapped at the old man during the meeting, perhaps the conversation might have been steered in the right direction. Now, the die was cast, and tension had built to an all-time high. The situation was out of control.

Anxiety caused his pulse to race, and he dropped a wrench. It clinked on the concrete floor and bounced under the workbench.

"Shit!" Wade bellowed.

Tension had built to the point where he was going to burst. There simply was no way out of the predicament. He shook his head at the sight of the wrench on the floor, with just one end showing.

Leaning over to retrieve it, he couldn't quite reach the tool. The bottom shelf impeded him.

Wade got down on his hands and knees, then he shoved an arm under the shelf. Wriggling with an outstretched hand, he fished around for the pesky wrench. Finally, he found purchase on the stray tool. Sliding it out, he inhaled, and a pungent odor whisked up his nostrils.

The scent was smokey, with a hint of melting plastic.

He looked towards the door and smoke billowed under the crack beneath it.

Wade had closed the door to keep the cold out. Now, he wondered how long he'd been in the room. *Couldn't have been more than fifteen or twenty minutes*, he thought.

Reaching for the doorknob, his fingers latched upon scorching hot metal.

"Crap!" he said, shaking his hand.

Wade inspected the damage. His fingertips were red, but they hadn't begun to blister.

He fetched a rag, then used it to turn the knob.

When he opened the door, a wave of smoke rushed into the storage room.

He stood at the threshold and couldn't see anything but blackness and gray. Considering the floorplan, he tried to decide how to get out. Things finally came into view. Flames wafted from floor to ceiling about the basement, burning the equipment and igniting the plank floor above.

Wade choked on fumes. Pulling his trucker's coat over his mouth and nose, Wade breathed through the thick lining. Then, he made his way through the basement.

The building was equipped with a freight elevator. They typically used it to move between levels. Wade thought better of getting in the rickety lift. Power could go out at any moment, leaving him stuck in the elevator, trapped to die of smoke inhalation.

He headed for a staircase. Zigzagging around the fire and machinery, he slowly navigated through the dense smoke. Flames erupted from different areas, as though gasoline had been poured in several locations. His eyes watered from the smoke, but he could see a discarded gas can near a foundation wall.

When he finally reached the stairs, Wade found Jenkins strewn on the floor.

He crouched beside the old-timer, trying to check for signs of life.

The old man's eyes were glazed over. Wade considered whether he should carry the man upstairs.

An explosion erupted behind him.

The electrical room had gone up in a blaze.

"The hell with this," he muttered.

Wade stood up and ascended the stairs, two at a time. Then, he ran across the factory floor, as flames whirled upward between gaps in the old planks. Smoke billed into the air, and exertion and warmth from the fire caused him to sweat. Beads of perspiration ran down his face.

He eventually made it to the door and stepped outside into the wintry night.

Letting go of his coat, Wade exposed his face to the cold air. He tilted his head back and breathed in deeply. He coughed a few times. Then, fresh air filled his lungs. Relief.

He trotted over to his truck, opened the door, and slid behind the wheel.

Starting the engine, he surveyed the gravel parking lot. There was another vehicle out there. *Jenkins' pickup truck*, he thought.

Everyone else had already gone. *Split before the worst of it.*

Wade shifted into drive, then he raced out of the parking lot, leaving the building engulfed in flames.

He sped down country roads, headed into the foothills of the Monadnock Region of southwestern New Hampshire. His truck climbed upward, headed towards his house in Lyndeborough. He raced from the scene of the fire, seeking to put distance between himself and the calamity.

Wade sought freedom, at least for the moment, while it could last.

CHAPTER FIVE

MASON WALTERS went fishing again. He trudged towards the riverbank and stood on shore for a moment, as frigid water dripped from his waders. This morning, he wore tan trousers, a white dress shirt and tie beneath his fishing gear. He was ready for the office.

He shook his head in disappointment. Mason had come up empty-handed.

He scanned the stream. The crisp autumn foliage that had reflected in the standing pools a week beforehand was replaced by views of snow-covered riverbanks. Mason contemplated whether the brook trout from last week might be the final catch of the year. Winter would be coming soon, and he didn't tend to venture out much after November.

Breaking down the fly rod, he slid the fiberglass shafts into an aluminum case, then he twisted the tube-cap into place. He shoved the reel into a cloth bag and pulled the drawstrings tight. And then, he slid out of his waders and tucked them and his wading boots into a nylon tote with mesh panels.

He stowed the gear in the back of his sporty Volvo wagon, pulled the luggage cover into place, then he shut the lid.

Sliding into the driver's seat, he tossed his Orvis ball cap onto the passenger seat. He hit the start button, then he turned on the controls for the heated seat and steering wheel.

Mason patted down his gray, thinning hair. Backing the car around, he then drove along a dirt road, lined with old stone walls. When he turned onto the macadam, he accelerated and whisked down the road. It ran along the Souhegan River, which meandered through a valley below.

He'd left his quaint house in Hollis, New Hampshire early that morning to get some fishing in before settling into a mundane paperwork day at the office.

Leaving the countryside, he turned onto a main roadway and encountered traffic. The street was packed with new office buildings, chain restaurants, and shopping plazas. Eventually, he turned right onto Main Street and the idyllic view of downtown Nashua lay before him.

Antique brick buildings lined both sides of the street, with occasional newer establishments lodged in-between them. Old-fashioned streetlamps were adorned with white lights and garland for the upcoming holidays.

He cruised down the wide roadway with parking on either side of the street, then he cut over to High Street and found a space on the third level of the municipal parking garage.

Mason climbed out of the car and opened the rear door. He pulled a coat off the back seat and wriggled into his Barbour waxed jacket, then he slung an Orvis backpack over his shoulder. It was filled with file materials, pens, phone and wallet.

Hoofing over to the office, he crossed Factory Street and stepped onto a narrow sidewalk. It was covered with a dusting of snow. Walking alongside an old brick building, he took his time being careful not to slip. Mason didn't have any pressing deadlines, and he relished the thought of an easy day.

Mason rounded the corner onto Main Street. The sidewalk along the major throughfare was wide and trimmed in brick. Flower beds with deciduous trees were draped in a light blanket of snow.

The building on the corner housed a barbershop, restaurant, and pharmacy on the ground floor, and professional offices on the second floor.

Mason approached the door leading to the second story of the Patriot Building. A marquee with the listing of the businesses on the second floor included the name of his law firm at the top. He opened the door and stepped out of the cold. His copy of the morning paper lay on the floor in the entranceway.

Scooping up the *The Telegraph*, he perused the top headline. It ran with a story about an insurance fraud arrest. A few mugshots were plastered under the opening article with the word *arson* written in bold letters. Mason shoved the paper under his arm, then he trudged up the staircase, lined with wood paneling.

Reaching a landing, he turned and walked towards an inner door, with a large window in the center trimmed in oak. A man stood in the hallway outside Mason's office, appearing anxious. He looked familiar, but Mason couldn't place him. Too many cases, too many people.

Opening the door to the upstairs suites, Mason nodded to the stranger. "Didn't realize I had an appointment this morning," he said, unlocking the door to his suite.

"You don't," the man said, nervously.

"Well, please tell me how I can help you," Mason said.

The man lingered in the hallway, diffident. He seemed unsure of what to say.

Mason stepped into the reception area of his suite.

A large room comprised the space, with an antique reception desk on one side of the room. The other side was furnished with a sleek black sofa, matching chair, and coffee table. Filing cabinets and a copy machine were situated behind the desk. Prints of the local landscape hung on the walls. Yesterday's newspaper and a few fly-fishing magazines were spread on the coffee table, which had a black top and chrome legs. The office had the feeling of a turn-of-the-century motif, with oak furniture, mixed in with a hint of modern, art deco items from a similar period.

Mason turned and faced the man standing in the hallway.

A desperate look crossed the man's face. "I was hoping you could help me."

"We usually only see people by appointment," Mason said.

The man's eyebrows furrowed with disappointment. And then, the man's worried look finally registered with Mason. The lawyer realized where he'd seen the stranger before. It had been in a mugshot plastered on the morning's paper.

CHAPTER SIX

"PERHAPS you should come in," Mason said, extending a hand. "I'm Mason Walters."

The man stepped into the reception area, appearing unsure of what to do. He dropped his head forward, like a turkey searching for a morsel on the ground.

He shook Mason's hand. "I'm Tyler Cummings. Thanks for agreeing to see me."

Tyler looked to be in his late thirties, hip with long, brown hair. He glanced around, as though wondering if he should sit down in the reception area while Mason got situated.

"You can take a seat right there for a moment," Mason said, motioning to the sofa. "I'll just be a minute. Then we can head back to our conference room."

Mason stepped through a small interior hallway area and walked into an office, located in the back left of the suite. A chair rail ran along all the walls, with the upper portion painted off-white and the lower portion was painted sage green. Plaques of his degrees and licensures ran along the left-hand wall, while mementos from his days in the Army were plastered on the right.

After his stint in the Army, he'd moved home and attended the University of New Hampshire, majoring in English. He focused on early British literature, especially Shakespeare. He had thought of graduate school and teaching at a college until he met his wife. Amelia also majored in English at UNH and had plans of becoming a high school teacher. Rather than go into teaching college, Mason decided upon law school, so he could live in New Hampshire. Their plans caused him to move out of the state to attend the University of Connecticut for law school, while Amelia hung on at UNH for a master's degree in teaching.

He set the newspaper on a black guest chair. The suite had high ceilings and two rooms with large windows overlooking Main Street. All the windows were adorned with wooden blinds.

He approached an antique oak desk and set his backpack on the floor, then he fished through it, pulling out a laptop computer.

A window behind Mason's desk was stenciled on the outside in gold leaf lettering:

> Mason P. Walters
> Attorney-at-Law

Setting the computer on the desk, he reached into the bag for his reading glasses and a pen. Then, he grabbed a business card from a pewter holder on the desk, and a notepad off the top of an oak filing cabinet.

Mason walked into the small hallway, separating the reception area from the other rooms. Two slatted doors were situated on the right, pulled open. A sink was housed in the space with a medicine cabinet above it. A chrome trashcan and blue recycle bins were located beneath the sink.

A coat closet was opposite the wash area.

"Shall I take your coat," Mason said, pointing to the closet.

Tyler shrugged. "I'm okay."

"You can step back here," Mason said, turning away.

Mason stepped into the room adjacent to his office. It was furnished as a conference room, with an oak library table in the center. Oak courtroom chairs were situated on one side, and an antique office chair with rattan backing was on the other. He pulled out a courtroom chair for Tyler, then he walked around the table and sat down.

Prints of various trout species and dry flies hung on the right-hand wall. A lateral filing cabinet with a laminated wooden top rest against the left. This room also had windows overlooking Main Street. A window was stenciled in large letters on the outside with the name of the firm and a phone number beneath.

The gold leaf lettering read:

Law Offices of Mason Walters
603-943-7761

Several cacti were potted and rest on the slate windowsill below the firm moniker. A few redwells, stuffed with file materials, were perched against a wall. Mason had a tidy office, but there were enough signs to show that he had a busy practice.

Tyler stepped into the conference room, looked around, then slid into the wooden chair. He seemed uneasy with the environment, despite the homey feel of the place.

Mason set the notepad down and slid a business card across the table.

Grabbing the card, Tyler placed it beside him.

"We'll get some coffee going in a few minutes," Mason said. "What brings you to see me?"

"You've seen this morning's paper?" Tyler glanced at the table, as if embarrassed.

"I've only scanned it." Mason shrugged. "Spent the morning in a river chasing trout."

Tyler looked at the wall adorned with prints. He nodded, understanding.

"Why don't you tell me what's going on?" Mason suggested. "Start from the beginning, so I get the background. The lay of the land so to speak."

"Sure." Tyler sat up. "I'm originally from the Midwest. Grew up in Wisconsin. I attended the University of Wisconsin and got a business degree. My brother moved out this way for college and borrowed money to buy an old mill building up in Charlestown, New Hampshire, along the Connecticut River. I started working there after college. I lived on the property. Saved some money."

"This all sounds fairly basic." Mason smiled, trying to reassure the young man.

"My brother's business was manufacturing lower end caskets, made from wood, particle board, and veneer laminate. These are for people who cannot afford expensive funerals."

"Yes, I'm familiar with them," Mason said.

"Well, I worked there for a few years. Saved a decent amount of money and met several people working in manufacturing."

"Tell me what brings us to the current predicament."

"I'm getting to that. Four of us went in together and purchased the Wilco Manufacturing Company, which is located in Wilton, New Hampshire. It manufactures component parts for industrial equipment," Tyler explained. "Each of us became twenty-five percent owners. We figured that division would make any important decision required to be unanimous."

"But that didn't hold true..." Mason offered.

"Things were fine at first. My brother's company bought certain parts, and we obtained an existing customer base when we bought the business. The prior owner sought to retire and didn't have any children interested in taking over the company. We got a note from a bank, and we offered the owner a promissory note on the rest."

"What was the purchase price?"

"Two million dollars..."

Mason considered the young man's comment. "You got yourself in debt for half a million dollars?"

He nodded. "That's just the start of it."

"There's more?"

"Yes. Two of the owners, Wade Garrett and Crystal Baker... Well, they were in a romantic relationship. This left me and Scott Bancroft out in the cold for most important decisions."

"The two shareholders could vote together and decide whatever they wanted," Mason said.

"Correct." Tyler edged to the table, intense.

"What exactly happened from there?" asked Mason.

"They began living an extravagant lifestyle." Tyler inhaled. "One that couldn't be supported by the business. It's the type of operation that could allow one or two owners to live comfortably. But it couldn't support four people living lavishly."

"Makes sense," Mason said, taking notes.

"Well, they contracted to build a huge house in Lyndeborough," Tyler said. "Crystal wanted to go on trips. Wade and Crystal were always away or buying things for the house. This left me and Scott doing a lot of the work."

"Moss didn't grow under their feet," Mason said.

"No, sir. It didn't." Tyler chuckled and showed the first sign of relief since he'd arrived.

"How did this impact the business?"

"They started taking out lines of credit, leasing expensive cars for all of us. And they drew salaries that dwarfed our incoming receivables."

"So, the debt grew?"

"The debt grew," Tyler confirmed.

"How much?"

"They had us in for close to a million each."

"On a business worth only two million."

"Correct."

"The newspaper noted an arrest for arson, which is usually an insurance scam. How could that bail you out when looking at these numbers?"

Tyler shrugged. "The bank loan was only 400,000 dollars. All the rest was owed to Herbert Jenkins, the prior owner."

"What was the building worth?"

"About 1.2 million."

"That would leave you with a net of 800,000 dollars," Mason said. "It would help with cash flow, but the business being out of commission due to a fire would prevent you from paying back Jenkins."

"We had a business owner's insurance policy with a lost profits provision in the event of a casualty."

"But that would only take you so far. I'm afraid I don't get the point of the scam."

"Mr. Walters," Tyler pled. "I am just giving you the background. To be clear, I'm not certain of the aspects of the scam myself."

"You didn't participate?" Mason asked.

"No, sir." Tyler shook his head. "But that's the least of my troubles."

"There's something more?" Mason sat back and looked him directly in the eyes.

Tyler nodded and said, "Jenkins is dead."

CHAPTER SEVEN

WADE GARRETT got released on bail and was too revved up to speak with an attorney right away. He needed to unwind. The girlfriend that he kept on the side would be just the right medicine.

Lexi really knew how to treat him right.

Wade slowly rolled up her driveway, the tires of his pickup crunching over snow covered gravel. He looked around for any indication of her boyfriend. No sign of the man's truck. Things looked quiet inside, but her Honda was parked in front of the barn.

Pulling in behind her car, he climbed from the cab of his truck and eased the door shut. He held a rag in his hand. Wade went around to the back of the truck and grabbed a fuel can from the cargo bed. He picked up the gas can with the rag to prevent leaving fingerprints on the can. Then, he walked over to the barn and pushed the sliding door ajar.

He stepped into the barn and couldn't see a thing. It took a moment for his eyes to adjust.

Light from a window near the hayloft reflected into the space below. Wade walked over to an old workbench, made of thick planks worn smooth at the edges from over a century of use. He set the fuel can down where he'd found it a few days beforehand.

Then, he eased out of the barn and gently slid the big door closed.

He shoved the rag into his pants pocket, then walked over and knocked on the side entry door to the house. Anticipation raced through his loins.

When Lexi answered the door, a surprised look crossed her face. It quickly changed to a pleased grin. "What are you doing here?" Lexi said, opening the door.

"Came to pay you a visit."

"A little matinee?" she said, laughing.

Her brunette hair was pulled back into a ponytail, and she looked like she'd just been cleaning. But her young, athletic build looked just fine.

A nice piece of ass, he thought.

Wade grabbed her by the waist and started kissing her, as he pushed into the house.

CHAPTER EIGHT

THE DOOR leading into Mason's suite creaked open and footsteps resounded in the reception area. Tyler glanced over his shoulder nervously.

"Relax," Mason said. "That's just my assistant, Diane."

"Oh." Tyler inhaled, leveling himself.

"The police won't track you to a lawyer's office."

"Didn't think so. Guess I'm just a little jumpy."

Rising from his chair, Mason went to greet his assistant but stopped at the threshold. "I'm going to fetch some coffee," he said to Tyler. "Do you want any?"

Tyler mulled it over, then shook his head. "No. Thank you, anyway."

Mason shrugged. "Suit yourself."

He walked into the reception area and found Diane getting situated behind her desk. She had worked with him for over twenty years.

"Morning," she said with a kind smile.

"How are you?" he asked.

"Great." And she seemed chipper.

Diane was in her early forties, fit, and wore a dress shirt, trousers, clogs, and a fleece vest. This was common attire for the office on days when appointments weren't scheduled, and typical for small, northern New England law firms.

When Mason didn't have court, a deposition, or a client meeting, he usually dressed in activewear, resembling a model from a fly-fishing outfitter. He preferred clothes from Orvis. Diane tended to follow his lead, except she opted for the L.L.

Bean look. However, Mason mixed it up with the occasional dress shirt, tie, and chinos.

Mason stepped over to the coffee maker and selected a dark roast, then he slid a mug into the machine. He hit a button and let the machine go to work. Dark coffee slowly dripped into the cup. Aroma from one of Peet's Coffee signature blends wafted into his nostrils.

He turned to Diane while he waited for the coffee to brew. "This smells good."

"Didn't know you had an appointment this morning," she said, sarcastically. Seated behind her desk, Diane flipped through documents and clacked on the keyboard to her desktop computer. It never took long for her to get started.

Mason shrugged. "We didn't," he whispered. "He was waiting here when I got in."

Diane rolled her eyes. She didn't care for people who couldn't follow the rules.

"Wonder how many people show up at a doctor's office without an appointment," Mason whispered to her.

"Probably none," she said.

The coffee machine spit out the last of the java into his mug. His cup was adorned with the logo of his old infantry unit. A patch of the Big Red One was plastered on the side of the cup. He took a sip of black coffee and it hit the spot.

"Good?" Diane asked.

"Definitely." He nodded.

"Maybe I'll grab a cup later," she said. "I prefer cream and sugar."

"I like my coffee black, hot, and made within the last six hours," Mason said.

They both chuckled at the allusion to a similar line from a pulp crime novel.

"Besides," he said. "I could really use it this morning."

"You hit the stream on the way in. Right?"

"Sure did. I'm still in need of warming up a bit."

Diane smiled, then turned back to the paperwork in front of

her.

Mason leaned over and opened the chrome door to a mini-fridge and grabbed a bottle of water. They kept a few on hand for client visits. Diane and Mason just used the water cooler, located in the corner near the sofa.

He walked back into the conference room and shut the door.

"Water?" he said.

Tyler nodded. "Sure."

Mason put the water down, then he slid open a drawer in the library table and pulled out a couple of coasters. Dry flies were printed on them. Tossing one in front of the prospective client, Mason then placed the bottle of water on it.

He slid the other coaster to his side of the table.

Stepping around the oak table, he set his coffee down on the coaster and took a seat. The chair creaked as he leaned back. The occasional hum from cars traveling down Main Street filtered through the dense walls of the old brick building.

The room was fairly quiet, and Tyler didn't seem to know what to say next.

Steam rose from Mason's coffee mug, and he let a moment pass before taking up the discussion. This was a tricky point in the relationship with a criminal defendant. An attorney must be careful of what a client reveals to him. The code of professional ethics prohibits counsel from allowing a client to introduce perjury into evidence. Hence, a statement made in a meeting can have longstanding consequences.

A client who admits to committing a crime during a conference with his attorney cannot later take the stand and say he didn't do it. Such an admission usually leads to the defendant not testifying at trial. Otherwise, an ethical lawyer is forced to withdraw if the client continues to insist on lying during his testimony.

"How did Jenkins die?" Mason finally said.

Tyler shrugged.

"You don't know?"

"No," Tyler said, shaking his head.

"How do you know he died?"

"The police told me."

"The police!"

"Yeah. What's wrong?" Tyler looked like a confused schoolboy.

Mason had gotten sidetracked. The surprise visit hadn't allowed him to ponder various angles or prepare for the meeting. He typically ferreted out important details early during an initial discussion with a client.

"Were you interrogated by the police?" asked Mason, while taking notes.

"I spoke to them," Tyler said, reaching for his water. He looked nervous, like it had just dawned on him that maybe he'd made a mistake.

Mason sighed. Tyler probably had said too much. But one could never know.

"Figured that I hadn't done anything wrong, so—"

"They arrested you, right?"

"Yes."

"Never talk to the police. It can only hurt you."

"Okay, got it."

"What did you discuss?"

"They asked me about the business background, like I've told you," Tyler said. "And they asked me a lot of details about my activities from last week."

"What did you tell them?"

"Basically, I explained that I live with my girlfriend in Milford. I was already at home around the time they say the fire started."

"So, you have an alibi. Why did they make the arrest?"

"Well, I had a spat with my girlfriend. She stayed at her mother's house that night, so she couldn't vouch for me."

Mason shook his head. "The police heard the business was in trouble. There was a fire. They suspect the business owners of arson. And you couldn't prove you weren't at the mill when the fire occurred. Typically, they make an arrest based upon

34

suspicion, then leave it to you to prove you're innocent."

"That's about it." Tyler shrugged.

"What has this Jenkins' death got to do with it?"

"I'm not a hundred percent sure." Tyler shrugged.

"What did they say to you?"

"Jenkins died on the night of the fire...under fishy circumstances."

"Like what?"

"They didn't say."

"You were only arrested for arson, right?"

"Conspiracy to commit arson."

"Not murder, though."

"No. Not murder."

"Any of the others?"

"My business partners?"

"Yeah. Your business partners."

"Not to my knowledge. Not for murder or arson. I think it's all just conspiracy to commit arson right now."

"But you think that might change?" Mason said.

Tyler nodded. "My guess...the guy died the night of the fire, and they are trying to track something down to show it's murder."

"Like what?"

"Hell if I know."

"What's the motive for someone killing Jenkins?"

"There was a life insurance policy on him, running in favor of the business."

Mason sat back. He figured something like that was in play.

It's often part of a business sale. The business is not readily marketable. An owner finds a few young people willing to step in, but they cannot finance the entire deal. The owner is older. Along with the sale there is an agreement to carry a life insurance policy on the prior owner, so when he eventually passes away, the balance of the loan owed to him is paid to his estate as a lump sum. Any remainder of the policy goes to the new owners.

"Makes sense. How much would you get, total?" asked Mason.

Tyler sat back, as though he were running the numbers through his head for the first time. "About $200,000, after paying off the mortgage with the fire insurance and Jenkins' estate with the life insurance."

"So, you're wiped clean of debt and walk away with a pot of cash?"

"Pretty much," Tyler said.

"And you haven't got an alibi, whatsoever."

"None. Except my partners likely knew I'd left the mill before the fire."

Mason's chair creaked as he leaned back. "Looks like you're in a bit of a pickle."

"How much will it cost me?" asked Tyler. "To hire you."

Mason ruminated for a moment. "A case like this, with arson and a potential murder charge…already media coverage on it, so the prosecution will be difficult to deal with. I'd need a $25,000 retainer."

Tyler shook his head. "How about $10,000?"

"This isn't a time to skimp. You're in serious trouble here," Mason said. "You could be looking at a long prison term. This case will need a private investigator and significant hearing and trial preparation. There will be times when I can't work on anything else."

"Okay. I can come up with $10,000 now," Tyler said. "I'll get the rest from my parents. It will take a few days."

"Why don't you give me copies of everything you have?" Mason said. "Bail conditions and any other paperwork you got from the police. We'll get you an engagement agreement drawn up before you leave."

Tyler fished some paperwork from his coat pocket and slid it across the table.

Grabbing the forms, Mason perused them. Standard arrest and release documents. "Anything else I need to know?" Mason said.

"Just that my girlfriend could be a bit of problem."

Mason wondered what kind of people this kid associated with.

CHAPTER NINE

MASON showed his new client to the door after they had taken care of the engagement letter and initial retainer payment. He reminded Tyler not to speak to the police if they came calling.

The kid seemed worried, and Mason felt bad for him. News like this wasn't like wine, it wouldn't get better with age. No matter what happened, the young man's life was changed forever. It typically took the shock of a situation to wear off before a client understood the long-term consequences of an arrest that gets into the daily rags.

After he closed the office door, Mason turned to Diane and shook his head. "Afraid that kid has a hard road ahead of him."

"You don't say," Diane replied. "His picture was plastered all over the news this morning. They're talking arson. Seems like a lot of hoopla for such a crime."

"Afraid I missed this morning's news broadcast."

"One would expect that to be the case, when one rises early to wander around in cold streams chasing after fish."

They both laughed.

He walked over and placed the executed engagement letter and the retainer check on the edge of her antique reception desk. It stood chest-high, with a top-piece that served as a ledge. There was a rolltop function that Diane seldom used.

The new client intake left him uneasy.

Mason walked across the reception area and sat down in a modern chair. Turning to Diane, he said, "I have a feeling this is going to end up being a lot worse than arson."

"Like what?"

"Murder."

CHAPTER TEN

WADE GARRETT pushed off his mistress, then fetched his jeans from the floor. Lexi stretched out on the bed, eyeing him as he zipped up his fly. The bedcovers were draped around her nude, lithe body, revealing curves and hints of flesh.

"Sure you don't want to go another round?" she said.

"Of course I do," Wade replied, grinning.

"Then why don't you come over here and take me one more time?"

Sexy Lexi had him aroused, but Wade thought better of it. There was too much going down. He was concerned about Tyler setting off on some quest for honesty, and the kid didn't have much common sense. Wade was worried Tyler might have already talked to the police. A naïve young kid, Tyler didn't know how to keep his mouth shut.

"We don't need your boyfriend finding out that I'm balling you," Wade finally said. "At least not right now."

She appeared let down by the comment. "I doubt he'd catch us," Lexi said.

Wade shook his head. "I'd bet money he's on his way here right now."

"He was going to meet with a lawyer in Nashua."

"Sure, but most lawyers don't take meetings without appointments. We just got bailed out. And besides, I seriously doubt if he got a meeting that it would last very long."

"Maybe…" Lexi said, but she didn't sound convinced herself.

He sat on the edge of the bed and slipped his boots on. Then, he tied the laces, slapped her leg, and stood to leave. "We'll have time soon enough. Maybe we'll slip off for a weekend, like before."

She smiled, pleased. "You promise?"

"Sure, honey. Anything for you."

Lexi sat up, and he leaned towards her. While placing a hand on her back, he gently squeezed her smooth skin. Then, he kissed her goodbye. A long, passionate kiss.

She fell back into a pillow. "Don't keep me waiting too long," Lexi said.

Wade caressed her leg, then he turned to leave. "See you, babe."

Pushing the storm door open, he headed for his truck and let the door slam shut behind him. The wooden door smacked loudly against the doorframe. She probably jumped at the sound. A harsh noise, meant to unsettle her.

He slid behind the wheel and smirked, proud of himself.

Wade had rough ways, and he liked how gentler folks were put off by him. Startling sounds, curt responses, chewing tobacco and vulgar language, it all served to keep people distant. It also made people afraid of him, and he relished their fear.

Banging a left onto Ponemah Hill Road, he pulled in front of an Audi bombing down the country road.

Probably a yuppie leaving the tennis club, he thought.

Wade looked in the rearview mirror and sneered at the driver behind him. Cutting the Audi off had caused the man to brake hard. The guy had likely met up for a late morning match. Now, the yuppie was anxious to get to his office, and Wade was delaying him.

The Audi began tailgating Wade's truck. Wade could see the tense look on the man's face.

He chuckled at the suit's anger. Slowing down below the speed limit, Wade sought to annoy the man even more.

The other driver shook his head, smacked the steering wheel, but he didn't dare flip the bird at a guy driving a pickup truck on a lonely country road. Not out here.

Stone walls ran along the roadside, and large pine trees filled the areas between farmhouses and large colonials. Wade was familiar with the surroundings, having grown up in the town. Eventually, he drove into an area where a few old farmhouses had been converted into condominiums.

Wade's mind turned back to the current predicament. He hit the gas, worried he'd pass Tyler on the kid's way home from the meeting at the lawyer's office in Nashua. Ponemah Hill Road was on the east side of Milford, and it wouldn't take Tyler long to get there.

Pulling away from the Audi, Wade drove past old houses converted into multi-family dwellings. Wade had bigger fish to fry than some yuppie leaving the tennis club.

A moment later, he drove through an area close to the main road, where the country road divided a cluster of small, singlewide mobile homes. Wade never understood why those people stuck around. If he were going to live in a trailer, he'd do it someplace warm, like Florida or North Carolina.

Wade's truck rolled to a stop at a T-intersection with Route 101A. It was a main throughfare, which ran into the center of town. An Italian restaurant was located across the street.

He glanced to the right. No sign of Tyler coming down the street.

Taking a left, Wade pulled onto the main road and headed into town. A feeling of relief rolled off him, like a large wave splashing over a swimmer. Wade realized he hadn't been breathing properly. A shortness in breath caused him to inhale and gasp for air. He leveled off and settled his emotions.

As he drove further away from Ponemah Hill Road, he moved safely away from any trouble with Tyler. This relaxed him. But he couldn't understand why he was so concerned about a wussy like Tyler.

Wade thought about it. *I don't need that kid pointing them at me*, he concluded.

CHAPTER ELEVEN

MASON WALTERS sat at the paneled oak desk in his office, perusing the documents the new client had given him. The papers were spread out before him. Something appeared off, but he couldn't discern what was missing from the standard forms.

Reaching for the newspaper, he read the article in detail. It covered how a few local businessmen had been arrested for arson. Like many articles about crimes, it was short on details and about as accurate as a blindfolded marksman. Many particulars noted in the piece were incorrect. Even the charge was wrong, noting arson instead of conspiracy to commit arson. There was a mistake about the bail conditions. Tyler had been released on personal recognizance bail, which meant he had paid $25. But the newspaper stated they were each released on a $10,000 bond.

He shook his head frustrated, then glanced back at the forms. They were the standard documents police departments typically hand out after an arrest. A pink charge sheet noted the crime: Conspiracy to Commit Arson, RSA 629:3.

"What's got you all in a tizzy?" Diane said, standing in the doorway.

"The newspaper talks about arrests for arson," Mason griped. "But our guy was only charged with conspiracy to commit arson."

"You know they never get it straight," Diane said, smiling. She held a steaming cup of coffee in her hand.

"That for me?" He indicated to the mug.

"Sure is." Diane walked into his office and put the cup down on his desk.

"You know it's not your job to fetch me coffee."

"Nobody's fetching you anything," Diane said. "It's fine to grab a coffee for someone when you're getting a cup for yourself. Mine's in the other room." She stood by the desk, taking a peek at the front page of the paper. "This one's going to get dicey, isn't it?"

"Seems that way to me." Mason took a sip of coffee. "That hits the spot."

Diane chuckled. "I figured after a morning in a cool stream, you could go for another cup."

"You thought right." He smiled at her.

She grabbed his empty cup and started for the door.

Mason returned to the papers on his desk.

Diane reached the doorway, then she turned back. "Why would they only charge him with conspiracy to commit arson?" she asked.

"The crime of conspiracy is generally articulated in a New Hampshire statute. If a person agrees to engage in a crime found under one of the criminal statutes, along with other people, then he is guilty of conspiracy if just one of them goes through with the crime."

"Our client didn't burn the building, right?"

"I doubt it."

"One of them mentioned doing it, and our client either agreed and backed out... or he quietly assented to it," Diane said. "Then someone went ahead with it."

"Tell me how the police would know our client was complicit?"

"One of them ratted to the police," Diane said.

"You would think so," Mason said, nodding in agreement.

"The guy that actually torched the building is going to be furious when he finds out."

"Indeed," Mason said. "Hope he doesn't blame his arrest on Tyler."

"That could be trouble," Diane said.

"Big trouble," Mason agreed.

CHAPTER TWELVE

MASON ate a sandwich while he continued working at his desk. Then he made copies of a few documents he'd been reviewing from the new matter. Documents in a legal file have a way of spreading about the place, like a bunch of ducks scattering from a fisherman walking along a shoreline.

After collecting the materials, he put on a coat and ballcap and left the office for an early afternoon coffee break. A brisk wind funneled down Main Street from the river. It was perfect weather for moving to Florida. The sidewalk had been cleared, and small piles of snow and ice were heaped in the flower beds and along the granite curbs.

Mason pulled up the collar to his Barbour jacket and yanked the brim of his wool ballcap lower. Trucking down the sidewalk, he made his way over the bridge, spanning the Nashua River. Old mill buildings lined both sides of the riverbanks. Most had been converted into loft apartments. A few ducks swam through the cold, turbid water, and a heron stood in the reeds by the shoreline.

He turned the corner by a church, then headed up Franklin Street. Entering a café located in a refurbished brick building, he then crossed the plank floor and stood by the register. Mason ordered a coffee, then found a seat at a table near a window overlooking the river.

Spreading out case materials on the table, he tried to get a handle on the new matter. The authorities weren't required to turn over the police report until after the probable cause hearing. All a lawyer may know at the start of the case is the charge and what he can learn from his client, which in this case wasn't much. Sometimes the charge itself is revealing, other times it's not.

Mason perused a copy of the statute on arson, trying to discern the reason why Tyler was only charged with conspiracy. He also needed to understand the potential exposure.

The statute for arson required that someone actually start a fire or explosion. So, if Tyler didn't start the fire, he might only be charged with conspiracy. The crime of arson could be charged as a felony or misdemeanor. If the fire was started to seek recovery of insurance money, the crime would be charged as a felony. It could lead to a prison sentence of up to seven years.

The penalty for a conspiracy to commit a crime is the same as the crime that was the object of the conspiracy.

Glancing at the charge sheet, it noted a Class B Felony.

Mason took a sip of coffee and glanced out the window. A group of ducks swam towards a marsh, where a couple of Canadian geese nested in the reeds. The ducks maneuvered through the dried grasses then huddled together. Lowering their bills, they shut their eyes, and the sun radiated on them.

Safety in numbers, Mason thought.

He considered the case further. Diane was right. Someone had already flipped and put the police onto Mason's new client. When it came to humans, it wasn't always safer to operate in groups. People have a tendency to turn on each other rather quickly.

Betrayal often comes from those close to a person, Mason thought.

***

MASON returned to the office building. Stepping from the sidewalk through the door leading to suites on the second floor, he immediately felt warmth and was happy to escape the elements.

He ascended the stairs and entered his suite. Mason found

Diane seated at her desk. "Hi," he said, while shutting the door. "Did I miss anything?"

She peered over the top-piece of the reception desk and grinned. Shaking her head in mock admonition, she said, "Did you forget your cellphone?"

"Nope," he said, patting his coat pocket. "Got it right here."

Mason walked over to her desk. He rested his elbows on the oak surface and eagerly waited to hear what she had to report.

"Well, I tried to reach you a few times," Diane said. "I called twice, and text messaged you."

"Must be on silent mode from this morning," Mason said, with an aloof shrug.

"I should have guessed. You don't like to scare the fish away."

"So, what's going on?" he asked.

"A big development in the new case," replied Diane. "The client called. You're going to have to drop everything and get out there."

CHAPTER THIRTEEN

WADE GARRETT drove into the center of Milford and came to a stop at an intersection, which led into Union Square. The locals called it the oval. An old-fashioned common in the center of town, it was shaped more like a triangle than a square or an oval. Three roads surrounded a large, grassy island with a bandstand in the middle.

Storefronts ran along each side of the three roadways. Most of the old buildings had clapboard siding and large windows. A few structures were built from brick, like the town hall, which towered over the center of town. It had a prominent clocktower, which housed a Paul Revere bell. The bell was one of twenty-three surviving bells cast by the New England patriot.

The usual establishments occupied downtown: greasy spoon joints, used clothing boutiques, a real estate agency, a law office, and a bicycle shop.

The bandstand was shaded by large maple trees, with the leaves turned yellow and orange from the brisk autumn weather. Sidewalks and crosswalks connected the three sides of the oval and ran across to the island. The sidewalks around the island were made of brick. Granite curbs and steps offset the brick walkways, and the benches found throughout the common were made from granite. Milford had been dubbed the Granite Town long ago due to the numerous stone quarries that were located in the town.

When the traffic cleared, Wade banged a right and headed over towards a diner with a red metal roof. The restaurant was situated alongside the Souhegan River, perched high above the rapid current on the edge of a steep granite block wall.

He found an empty perpendicular parking spot and whipped his truck into it. All the parking spots were set at a slight angle due to the roads around the oval being one-way.

Wade climbed out of the cab and slammed the door shut, not bothering to lock it.

A gust of wind blew into his cheeks, and the muffled sound of water pounding over a dam resonated in the distance. He didn't pay for parking.

He stepped over a clump of snow, then walked towards a red door leading into the diner.

Wade stepped inside. As he closed the door, the din of clanging silverware and patrons chattering about current events supplanted the river flow that droned on outside. A television blared the local news in the background.

People glanced at the newcomer, stared for a moment, then returned to their meals and discussions. Everyone continued on like Wade hadn't even walked into the room.

Wade strode past customers huddled on stools at the counter and seated snug in booths. Nobody greeted him, despite Wade being a regular, who often joined in the late morning banter.

Taking a seat on a stool at the end of the counter, Wade tucked himself near a window overlooking the river below. He grabbed a menu and fiddled with it, passing the time until Dan got a break from the grill and came over to wait on him.

The menu had selections he'd never considered before. Wade usually just ordered the special. Dan offered pancakes, French toast, and every manner of cooking eggs.

Wade knew what he wanted to order, but the looks on people's faces made him feel awkward. He sought to avoid them, so he continued to check the options. He pretended to keep reading the menu and thought about how quickly things had played out. The arrest happened way too fast. Something had gone sideways. *A rat,* he thought.

A moment later, a coffee cup clanked on the counter and

stirred Wade out of his thoughts. He looked up to find Dan pouring coffee into the cup. The owner didn't seem happy to see him this morning. Dan was a burly man. He wore a white T-shirt and loose-fitting khakis, and he had an apron folded and wrapped around his waist, just under his potbelly.

"Know what you want?" asked Dan.

"Guess I'll just stick with the special," Wade said, shoving the menu between a napkin dispenser and a bottle of ketchup.

"Some things don't change, I guess."

Wade had the feeling Dan had just gotten in a dig, like he'd sensed the browsing of the menu had just been a ruse. "Well, I *am* going to change things up," Wade said, pointing at the menu. "You've got some good things in there."

"Thought you were going with the special, like always."

"Yeah, but this time I'm going to mix things up a bit. I'm gonna add an orange juice to the mix."

Dan pulled a notepad out of his pocket and reached for a pencil tucked behind an ear. He smirked, as though he wasn't amused with Wade's little charade. Dan jotted down the order and nodded. "Coming up," he said, coolly. Then, he turned away.

Wade glanced around. He caught the regular customers sneaking an occasional peek at him. They seemed to ponder him with keen interest, but they all turned away when Wade met their stares. Attention wasn't unusual for Wade. He relished it. But this type of scrutiny was something else altogether. He didn't like it.

He took a deep breath and tried to level his emotions. Wade was tough and typically handled pressure well. He was grace under fire. This was making him lose his nerve, though. And he didn't particularly care for it. This feeling of... vulnerability. Weakness.

Wade took a sip of coffee. Then, he reached into his coat pocket and fished out his phone.

Somehow this thing has gotten out, he thought. But he wasn't sure exactly how.

An arrest doesn't typically hit the papers so fast. He

reluctantly checked the digital edition of the local newspaper. The *Milford Cabinet* hadn't run a story, which was just what he expected. They went to print in the evening, well before this story could get out in the next morning's paper.

Then, he checked the *Union Leader* and got the same result.

Dan returned and slid a plate in front of Wade. It was loaded with eggs, toast, bacon, and hash browns. Then Dan placed a glass of orange juice beside the plate.

"Looks good," Wade said, forcing a smile.

Dan didn't reciprocate. He just nodded and said, "Top off your coffee?"

"Sure thing." But Wade wasn't totally sure about anything right now.

Stepping over to a Bunn coffeemaker, Dan picked up a fresh pot. Then, he trundled back to Wade and poured more coffee into the cup.

"What gives?" Wade snapped.

"Not sure what you're talking about."

"Them," Wade said, motioning towards the regulars.

"You've got a problem with them... I suspect you might want to talk to *them*. Afraid I can't help you."

"Well, I'm asking you!" Wade snapped, partly rising from the stool.

Dan shook his head. "Now you listen here. You're not captain of the team anymore. In fact, you haven't been for quite some time. So, you've got no cause to be talking to me that way."

Wade was taken aback. Dan had never stood up to him before. "It's just that—"

"I'm not looking for an explanation," Dan said. "You need to lower your tone. That's all."

Wade shrugged. There was nothing left to say. He wasn't going to learn anything from Dan. The guy held a grudge from their old high school football days. Wade had been a linebacker and a co-captain on the team. Dan was a nose guard, who had always played hard but never got much recognition. And he never got the girls.

Sitting alone, Wade ate his eggs and mopped up the yoke with his toast. He wolfed down the meal due to hunger and because it gave him something to do. The food helped settle his queasy stomach.

They all know, he thought. Somehow, it had gotten out.

***

WADE had about cleaned his plate. He took a sip of coffee, then figured Dan might be right about asking someone what the hell was going on. Wade wanted to know. Heck, he *needed* to know.

I'll just ask one, he concluded. *But which one?*

Scoping out the regulars, Wade spotted Jedediah Haywood at a booth nearby. Jed had his back to Wade and was talking to a couple of older men. Wool hunting jackets were piled on the bench seat beside Jed. He wore bib overalls, and he had a long, flowing gray beard.

Jed knew the bible from cover to cover. He read obscure books, like early American literature and Shakespeare. He also kept up on current affairs, politics, and local news. A copy of the latest edition of *Field & Stream* was often set on the table or counter next to him. Retired from working as a supervisor at a granite quarry, Jed tended to hang about the diner and talk to anyone who would listen. He picked up tidbits of information, too. If anyone had the scoop on Wade's predicament, Jed would be the one to know.

"Hey, Jed," Wade politely called over.

Nobody responded. Wade couldn't tell if they hadn't heard, or whether they were just plain ignoring him.

Leaning towards the men in the booth, Wade spoke louder, "Hey, Jed. You got a minute?"

One of the hunters lifted his chin, acknowledging Wade. Then he muttered something to Jed, while pointing at Wade.

Wade had no idea what the man had said. He was about to repeat the request when Jed slowly turned and peered over his shoulder at him. A cold, stern look accompanied Jed's gaze, as if the old-timer were sizing him up.

Looking away for a moment, Wade took a swig of coffee. Maybe he didn't really want to know what Jed had to say. Then Wade took in a number of the regulars, staring at him with contempt in their eyes.

I've got to know what the hell is going on.

"Hey, Jed?" Wade called. "Have you got a moment?"

"Sure. I've got a moment," Jed replied. "Just not sure if I've got the time for you."

"I'd really appreciate a minute of your time," Wade said. "Please."

Jed begrudgingly shook his head, as though he didn't want to come over. Then, he got up with a coffee cup in hand.

He walked over with a doleful expression on his face. It seemed like he really didn't want to talk. Not to Wade anyway. Wade had gotten along pretty well with Jed in the past. He'd never wronged the man, so he couldn't understand the reluctance to speak.

Was it that bad? Wade wondered.

Taking a seat on the stool beside Wade, the codger raised his coffee cup and forced a smile. He took a long sip, then stared Wade directly in the eyes. "So, what do you want?"

The man's eyes were penetrating. Jed was the kind of guy that didn't always reveal his thoughts; he didn't say everything that was on his mind. Wade tended to spout off when he got upset with someone. Folks like Jed made him uncomfortable. They *knew* things.

"Just wanted to know what was going on?" Wade finally said.

"You should know better than anyone else."

"Guess, I'd like to know what you've heard. That's all."

Jed nodded, understandingly. It was like he felt it was a fair question. "I've heard a few things..."

Wade didn't respond. He just let that sit there and waited until Jed had more to say.

"They ran a story in Nashua's *The Telegraph* about how you three boys got picked up for arson," Jed said, stroking his beard.

"There was a quick piece on Channel 9, too."

"Figured that it had gotten out there somehow," Wade muttered.

"Heard you were behind on payments to Herbie Jenkins," Jed said, eyeing him for a response.

Wade kept quiet. He wasn't about to lend credence to rumors about his business.

Jed took a sip of coffee, and said, "A few first responders were in here earlier this morning. They'd got overheard talking…"

"And?"

"Herbie Jenkins died."

"Died?" Wade wasn't entirely surprised to hear this.

He pictured Jenkins lying on the factory floor, and the mill ablaze as Wade ran for safety. Wade had kept quiet when he was arrested, so the police hadn't told him anything, and he hadn't revealed any facts to them, either. Loose lips sink ships. He wanted to keep his cards close to his vest, so he acted like Jenkins dying was all news to him.

"Yup." Jed took another sip of coffee and considered Wade carefully. The old-timer was trying to size up Wade. He was looking for hints of guilt.

"When?" asked Wade.

"Last night."

"How?"

"Probably in the fire you supposedly started," Jed said, turning to face Wade.

A wave of fear washed over him. Wade couldn't breathe. He remembered seeing Jenkins on the floor when he ran out. But Wade hadn't been certain of the man's condition, dead or alive, and wasn't about to wait in the flaming building to find out.

"They're saying he died from the fire?" Wade finally asked.

"Now, hold up," Jed said, raising a hand.

Wade leaned closer to Jed. Anxiety had him flummoxed and he lost his bearing. "You don't tell me what to do!"

Jed glared at him. "You want to hear this or not?"

"Sorry," Wade said, nodding. "Didn't mean to cut into you

like that."

"They haven't determined the cause of death. But they think it's likely due to the fire..." Jed considered his next words carefully. "Heard they're already considering bumping up that arson charge up to murder."

And with those words, Wade's entire world came ripping apart.

CHAPTER FOURTEEN

MASON had gotten the client's address from Diane. Then he drove to Milford, which is located over towards the southwestern part of the state. Crossing the town line, he drove past a vacant building on the left, where a family restaurant used to be located. A short ways after that, he drove past an Italian restaurant.

A developer had razed a historic farmhouse in order to build the Italian restaurant. A barn attached to the old house had once been used for a tavern called the White Horse Inn. The White Horse Inn had operated as a restaurant and bar. Many clients had come to Mason over the years after engaging in shenanigans there. He'd handled several assault and battery cases and a bunch of DUI matters for patrons of the famed tavern.

Back in the mid-1970s, a woman who had worked as cook and baker for the White Horse Inn had been associated with Sharon Tate's murder. Linda Kasabian had grown up in Milford and moved back to the town after being implicated in the Manson Family Murders. She was the driver of the car that transported the cult to Sharon Tate's house. Kasabian reported hearing the victims' screams as she waited in the car. She'd been given immunity to flip on members of the family. Kasabian had taken a job at the White Horse Inn, while trying to move on with her life.

She relocated and the tavern eventually closed. The developer who bought the property initially planned to run a restaurant out of the barn. But the plan got nixed after teenage arsonists burned the barn down.

Sometimes properties aren't torched for insurance money, Mason thought.

Mason turned left and headed up Ponemah Hill Road. He drove up the country lane and continued thinking about how fires can be started by people who don't even have an interest in the property. Sometimes they were caused by accident through electrical issues. Other times, its kids playing with matches.

Rounding a bend, Mason spotted Tyler's home without ever having been there.

A contingency of emergency vehicles was parked in the driveway and jumbled along the roadside.

Mason pulled to the soft shoulder, then he climbed out of his Volvo wagon. *This is getting to be quite an active case,* Mason thought. *Maybe I should have passed on it.*

He donned a ballcap and headed over to investigate.

His lowcut Barbour wellies crunched over the snowy gravel driveway.

Scanning the sea of police officers swarming the house, he tried to find someone he knew, or at least an officer who resembled the person in charge. A young couple was huddled together near the barn door. Tyler and his girlfriend stood by despondently, as they watched officers come and go from the house and barn.

Various officers carried items to a crime scene van. The Milford police were everywhere, and a few Wilton police officers accompanied them. Moving about the place, the cops didn't seem to be keeping to any boundaries.

Mason shook his head, expecting they were seizing more possessions than authorized by a search warrant. He approached a young officer, and said, "Who's in charge?"

The officer glanced Mason over, looking him up and down, as though trying to decide if he would even respond to the newcomer on the scene.

"I'm that man's lawyer," Mason said, pointing to Tyler.

"Good for you." The officer smirked, indicating he wasn't impressed with lawyers.

"Who's in charge?" Mason insisted.

"Sergeant Walsh," the officer replied.

"Where can I find him?"

The young cop pointed to a small group of officers; they were huddled on a patch of snow-covered yard near the front door.

Mason approached. But they didn't acknowledge him until he was standing beside them.

An officer looked at him, peeved. "You mind?" the officer said.

Ignoring the rude officer, Mason turned to the oldest one in the bunch. The man had dark hair with gray sideburns and ruddy cheeks from the cold. "Sergeant Walsh?" asked Mason.

"That's me," Walsh said. "What do you want?"

"I'd like to see a copy of the warrant."

"You what?" the rude officer interjected.

Walsh stepped towards Mason. "Just a minute," he said to the group.

"I'm Mason Walters, I represent—"

"Yeah, I know who you are," said Walsh. "How can I help you?"

Walsh's words conveyed an openness towards assistance, but his tone reflected guarded suspicion. Mason paused before answering. He considered the man.

Probably is accustomed to attorneys being forceful, Mason thought.

"You have a search underway," Mason said.

The rude officer stepped closer to him, and said, "Listen to captain obvious, here."

A few of the officers chuckled. The sergeant didn't.

"Captain obvious," the cop repeated. Then, he stepped forward to slap a buddy on the arm and lost his balance by stepping on a rock that had been hidden under the snow. His arms pinwheeled while he tried to regain his balance.

"Nice play, Shakespeare," Mason said to him.

The rude cop looked confused. "What?"

Mason directed his attention to the sergeant. "You have the

warrant?"

"Yeah…" Walsh said.

"Mind if I see the warrant?" asked Mason.

The sergeant frowned. Then, he dug the warrant out of his coat pocket. "Here you go," Walsh said, handing it over to Mason.

Mason read the document carefully. It allowed for the collection of electronics, such as computers and cellphones. The judge had also authorized a search of the barn.

Glancing through windows into the house, Mason spied officers ransacking the place. "Your officers are going way beyond the bounds set by this warrant," Mason said with an even tone.

Walsh bit his lip and shook his head. "This is a standard search."

"I'm going to have to ask you to instruct your officers to clear out of the house. They already seem to have the computer equipment," Mason said, pointing to the van. "They can search the barn. Then they have to go."

The rude officer sneered at him. "You can't tell us what to do!"

"I'm not," Mason said. "A judge already set the parameters for your search. If you don't like it, you can talk to him. And if you don't follow his instructions… well, I'll certainly take it up with him."

The group of officers stood there for a moment, eyeballing him.

Walsh was peeved. He finally shook his head, then called to the officers in the house. "Okay, let's concentrate our search on the barn."

The comment appeared like a change in course of action for tactical reasons, rather than following an admonishment from a criminal defense lawyer. Mason had seen this approach used before. A change in direction without admitting the mistake. It was meant to save face in front of the cops. Walsh had a tough guy image to preserve.

Officers funneled out of the house and converged on the

barn.

A few minutes later, a young female officer stepped out of the barn holding a gas can. She wore rubber gloves and was careful to only touch it in a couple places. "There's not much left in it," she said to Walsh.

"Bag it and tag it," Walsh said to her.

Then, he looked at Mason and grinned. "Looks like your boy will have to come back to the station."

Mason figured he knew why, but he asked the question anyway. "What for?"

"We may have to up his charge to a straight arson."

"Over a gas can found at his house?" Mason said. "Every barn and garage in the state has a gas can or two lying around."

"That one matches a gas can found at the scene," Walsh said. "An exact match."

CHAPTER FIFTEEN

WADE GARRETT wolfed down the rest of his breakfast, while sipping coffee and occasionally taking a swig of orange juice. Then, he tossed some cash on the counter and slipped into his denim trucker jacket.

He quickly walked through the diner towards the exit. A scent of grease wafted from the grill. His swift movements caught the attention of many patrons. But Wade didn't pay them any mind. He was pissed off. And when he got mad, he didn't tend to care what people were thinking.

They can go fuck themselves, Wade thought.

Pushing the door open, he stepped into the cold and stood on the sidewalk facing his truck. Something caused him to pause.

Rather than climb into the cab, he turned and crossed the busy street.

Wade marched up the sidewalk, passing storefronts that overlooked the oval. He slowed near a building with the words Law Offices stenciled across a plate-glass window. Then, he stepped into a recessed entryway and swung a heavy, wooden door open.

Inside, he approached a young woman seated at a desk in the reception area. She looked up at him quizzically.

"Kyle in?" Wade asked.

"Mr. Wentworth only takes meetings by appointment," she replied.

"Well, this here's kind of an emergency," Wade said, raising his voice.

"I'm afraid—"

A creek on the plank flooring caused her to break off in mid-sentence. Wade looked over and found Kyle Wentworth standing in the doorway leading from the reception area into his office.

The handsome thirty-five-year-old lawyer had held it together quite well. He sported a square jaw and athletic build, which carried over from his old playing days on the local high school football team. Wade had seen him play and expected the kid would land on a good college team. Instead, the kid went to a local university and studied hard to get into law school.

Kyle had a competitive spirit, and Wade liked that in an attorney. It was the reason he'd chosen to head over to the small law office located off the oval, rather than hire an attorney from one of the city firms.

"That's all right, Nancy," Kyle finally said, with an even tone.

"Sorry to barge in," Wade said, stepping towards the office.

"I kind of figured you might come by." Kyle motioned for him to enter.

There were two oak banker's chairs situated in front of an old-fashioned desk.

Wade walked in and sat down in the one closest to the door.

After shutting the door, Kyle stepped around the desk and took a seat in a big desk chair. He glanced across at Wade, sort of studying him before saying anything further.

Wade sat up straight. "Suppose you're wondering why I'm here?"

"I know exactly why you're here," Kyle said.

"You do?"

"Sure. The question is why are you coming to me?" Kyle said. Then he sat back waiting for the explanation.

"Figure we go way back, so to speak." Wade shrugged. "Both grew up in the same town, and we played for the same football team. Different years, but we chewed the same ground. I wanted to turn to someone tough, and someone I could trust."

Kyle nodded, as if understanding. "Makes sense. But a lot of times, folks in this type of situation seek legal counsel from a lawyer out of town. They hire a hotshot from Manchester, Concord, Boston, maybe even just bring in someone from over in Peterborough."

"I don't want to hire some stranger," Wade said, shaking his head.

"A stranger can be a good thing when it comes to criminal defense. Hiring a lawyer that doesn't know you allows the lawyer to be objective. He can assess the matter from a neutral viewpoint and advise on whether to take a plea deal."

"I ain't takin' no plea deal," Wade said, raising his voice.

Kyle didn't flinch. He just sat there as if waiting for Wade to calm down, reel in his emotions.

"Sorry," Wade said. "Just this thing has me a little wound up."

"As I recall, it isn't too hard to get you wound up," Kyle said, coolly.

"You gonna help me or not?"

"Tell you what," Kyle said. "We'll handle this discussion as a confidential communication. If for some reason I don't take this matter, then I promise I won't reveal anything from our discussion. And I won't represent anyone else involved."

"Sounds fair," Wade said, easing up a bit. "What you want to know?"

There was a lull in the discussion. Wade glanced around the room. It seemed fitting for a young lawyer in a small town. Kyle had an oak desk and chairs, and a couple of oak filing cabinets. There were a few oak bookcases with glass doors. Law books were crammed into the shelves. A few knickknacks were set on top of the bookcases, and a game winning ball was perched in the center of it all.

Nobody had ever given Wade a game winning ball, and he thought there were quite a few games his team won due to his efforts. He *deserved* a game ball.

He scanned the degrees, bar license, and federal court admission certificates. Kyle had accomplished a lot in his life. More than just money. The guy had set goals and kept a focus in order to achieve them.

Probably wasn't easy, Wade thought. *Plenty of distractions in college... girls and partying.*

Kyle was a straight shooter, but Wade decided to trust him.

"Why don't you start from the beginning?" Kyle finally said.

Wade explained how the business had gotten formed with his business partners. He discussed the loans and insurance coverages. Then, he admitted that they'd fallen behind on their finances. After explaining all this, he sat back in his chair and watched the lawyer's reaction.

"Did you torch the place?" Kyle said, watching him closely.

"Nope."

"Were you involved in burning it?" Kyle said.

Wade shook his head. "No, I wasn't."

"You've been arrested for conspiracy to commit arson, right?"

"That's correct. But I didn't do it."

"You don't have to be the one to light the fire in order to be arrested for conspiracy," Kyle explained. "You just have to agree to a plan to do it."

"That's messed up."

"Why do you say that?" Kyle said.

"You mean to tell me that if someone happens to talk about planning to burn a building, not intending to carry it out... they could go to jail for conspiracy, even if they didn't burn the building?"

"That's correct."

"What if they changed their mind?"

"Did you have that sort of discussion?"

"Might have..."

CHAPTER SIXTEEN

MASON WALTERS watched the female officer carry the gas can over to a crime scene van. It bounced off her thigh and caused her to lean this way and that, resembling an owner being pulled by a dog on a leash.

She shoved the can into a huge plastic bag, then jotted something down with a Sharpie.

"Hey," Walsh called to Mason. "We need to bring the kid down to the station."

Mason waved for Tyler to approach. The kid looked over at him, confused.

The rude cop smirked at Mason, apparently pleased with the development.

"You win a free ice cream cone?" Mason said to the cop.

Tyler Cummings didn't plod over. Instead, he remained standing next to his girlfriend near the barn door, apparently unsure what to do.

Walsh nodded to a couple of officers.

The cops walked towards Tyler, and he remained planted in place.

An officer pulled out a set of handcuffs and reached for Tyler's wrist. The kid called to Mason, "What's going on?"

"You're under arrest for arson," the officer said to him.

"What?" Tyler shook his head. "I've already been arrested."

Mason trucked over to his client. "You were charged with conspiracy. Now, they are planning on charging you with arson."

"Why?"

"They say there are matching gas cans," Mason said in a

hushed tone. "One at the scene, and one in your barn. This makes them think you lit the fire."

"But I didn't do it."

The officer eased Tyler's arms behind his back, and Tyler complied without resisting.

"Don't say another word," Mason advised him. "We'll talk after they've booked you."

Tyler nodded, understanding the need for silence.

The officer clicked the cuffs on Tyler's wrists, then checked to make sure they were secure.

Both officers held Tyler by his upper arms, then they escorted him towards a cruiser. Tyler's face was locked in a state of bewilderment; naivete apparently left him unable to grasp the situation.

One of his business partners set him up, Mason thought.

Boots crunched over the snowy gravel as the officers led Tyler along. The cop that had cuffed Tyler read his rights to him. Then, they cut across the snow-covered front lawn, and shoved Tyler into the back of a police cruiser.

A sullen look remained on Tyler's face, as he glanced out the window.

Tyler's gaze went past a group of officers and beyond Mason.

Mason turned to see what Tyler had fixated upon.

The lawyer followed his client's line of vision. Tyler had trained his focus on his girlfriend, who stood near the barn door with a disinterested look on her face. It seemed like she wasn't moved or even concerned about the turn of events.

CHAPTER SEVENTEEN

WADE GARRETT watched Kyle's reaction. It wasn't pleasant. The lawyer seemed to cringe at the admission to a link with a conspiracy to commit arson. The lawyer likely thought Wade was into this knee-deep. Arson. Murder. The whole nine yards.

Probably shouldn't have mentioned that, Wade thought.

"You need to understand," Kyle said after a moment. "An attorney cannot permit a client to take the stand and lie. So, anything you say to me can impact how we handle your case."

"Meaning?"

Wade had been in a few scrapes. He'd heard all this before. But he needed to flesh out how Kyle would handle things. Clarification was in order before he tossed money into representation. He didn't want to put a bunch a money into a lawyer, only to have to retain another one before trial. Wade wasn't good at school, but he was street smart; and, he certainly wasn't a fool.

"Meaning that you can't admit something to me, then say something different on the stand," Kyle said. "You've just admitted to at least thinking about conspiring to commit arson."

"Thinking about it and doing it are two different things," Wade snapped.

"I'm afraid it doesn't take too much thinking about a crime for the prosecution to put a conspiracy case before a jury."

Wade didn't like the sound of that. He appreciated Kyle giving it to him straight, though.

"Let's walk through this in a little more detail," Kyle said.

"The cat's already out of the bag. Tell me about this discussion."

"Wasn't much to it," Wade said, shrugging. "The three of us partners were talking about being behind on the loan. Orders were down. It was mostly a discussion about going to Jenkins and asking him for more time."

"How did the arson come up?"

"I told them if we couldn't get more time, maybe we should torch the place. This was said as a joke. Honestly, I figured Jenkins would agree to work something out. I mean... what else was he supposed to do?"

"Explain that last part."

"Sure. He was getting money from us." Wade sat up. "Not all of it. But he was getting something. If he called in the loan, our operation would shut down. That place would just sit there for at least a couple years. Jenkins wouldn't make a dime and he'd be straddled with overhead while it sat there, taxes, insurance, minimal heat. You name it."

"You think he would have gone along with a workout?"

"No telling for sure," Wade said. "He's an onery old coot. But he should have, though."

"Seems like it would make sense for him to go along with a workout. But now the place is burned, and Jenkins is dead. Doesn't look good."

"I'm thinking that someone had a beef with Jenkins," Wade said. "They wanted him dead. Maybe knew about our loan situation and set this whole thing up."

"That could explain the fire and the death... if Jenkins was murdered."

Wade smiled, feeling more assured by the lawyer's comment. *If Jenkins was murdered,* he liked the sound of that. *If,* he thought, almost saying it out loud.

Glancing around the office again, Wade took in the oak desk and chairs, as well as the oak bookcases with glass fronts. He looked at the degrees that hung on the walls in nice frames. Everything in the office was neatly arranged. Kyle wasn't overloaded with work. Probably took just enough cases to live a decent life. *Must be nice*, Wade thought.

"But how do you explain your conspiracy to commit murder charge?" Kyle said.

The comment took Wade by surprise. It made him sit back and think.

Kyle stared at him, waiting for a response.

Wade felt his own face contort from a smile into a frown. His pulse raced with fear. "Someone had to have ratted me out," Wade finally said.

Kyle nodded. "That's usually how these things work."

"How else would the police know I'd mentioned torching the place?" Wade said, shaking his head, dismayed. "That's what they based this charge upon, right?"

"Probably," Kyle said. "Look, I don't know all the angles just yet, so I can't say anything for sure. But you mentioned torching the place, and now we find you with a conspiracy to commit arson charge. They didn't charge you with arson... at least not yet. So, my guess is that someone must have said something. Now, who could that be?"

"That's a damn good question," Wade said.

***

WADE sat back and listened to the lawyer explain the elements needed to prove a conspiracy charge. Kyle told him that a defendant doesn't need to participate in a crime in order to be found guilty. Merely agreeing to a plan could be enough.

"You made the comment about burning the building in front of two business partners, right?" asked Kyle.

Wade nodded. "Had to be one of them."

"Not necessarily." The lawyer sat back and steepled his fingers. "One of them could have made a deal with the police. Maybe plea bargained for immunity. On the other hand—"

"What?" Wade demanded.

"One of them could have mentioned it to someone else. Perhaps someone with an axe to grind against you, or all three of you."

"Never thought of that," Wade said, inhaling.

He considered Tyler's girlfriend and wondered if she'd just used him to hatch a plan of revenge. Wade thought about his own girlfriend and business partner. Maybe Crystal had learned about Wade's extra-curricular activities. Crystal could have decided to move on and would want to be free of the business obligations with some cash in her pocket. She was an owner in the business and hadn't been charged, at least not to his knowledge. But he'd never mentioned the discussion to her.

"You're thinking who could have dropped the dime," Kyle said.

"Sure am," Wade replied, nodding.

"Any thoughts?"

"Plenty." Wade cracked a sly grin. "An old tomcat like me can make a lot of enemies. If you know what I mean."

Kyle nodded. "Sure do."

A lull fell over the discussion. Kyle didn't seem to like him much.

Wade thought about how no matter what he'd accomplished in life, there was always someone ready to look down on him. Knock him down a peg. He'd made captain of the football team. Then, he went on to run a few successful businesses. Heck, the recent setbacks could have happened to anyone.

"What's it going to cost me?" Wade said after a moment.

"A case like this…" Kyle shrugged. "It can get complicated."

"So, how much?"

"Well, I charge 235 dollars an hour. A misdemeanor requires a 10,000-dollar retainer, and a felony like this needs a 25,000-dollar retainer. It's pretty standard."

"Really?" Wade took a deep breath.

Kyle stared at him from across the desk. The lawyer didn't flinch.

"Can't we work out a down payment, with a payment plan?"

"No," Kyle said, shaking his head.

"Why not?"

"Think about the worst-case result. People in prison can't

pay outstanding legal bills."

"So, you think we're going to lose?"

"I'm not saying that," Kyle responded, flashing a politician's smile.

"That's good to hear," Wade replied, relaxing a bit.

"We seem to have a lot to work with here, if you're playing it straight with me," Kyle said. "That means that I have to sink some time into this, which is time that won't go into other cases. I'll be short on revenue if I didn't charge you the going rate. And I have to think about worse case scenarios. Otherwise, I'd lose my shirt."

"I think I understand," Wade said.

"Lawyers simply aren't willing to absorb the burden of any risk associated with mounting legal fees in a criminal case."

Wade thought about monies in a business account. "I can get it," he said.

The politician's smile returned. "Great," Kyle said.

"I'll be back within an hour."

"We'll have an engagement letter ready for your signature."

Kyle stood up and reached across the old desk. They shook hands.

Then, Wade turned and marched out of the building. Hurrying towards his truck, Wade hoped someone hadn't already cleaned out the account.

***

WADE hadn't gotten far when a caravan of police vehicles rolled into the oval. Two SUVs and a cruiser sped into the center of town from Nashua Street, whipping around the town common like they were on official police business. Heck, it looked like a presidential motorcade.

The procession drove past the outlet road leading to Route 13 and continued around the oval. Although the cars weren't flashing blue lights or blasting sirens, they moved at such a pace that it had caught people's attention. They weren't cars creeping along while on patrol with officers searching for something to do. Instead, they moved deliberately. Wade forgot about getting to the bank for a moment.

Seated in the back of a cruiser was a familiar looking person.

As the police cars drove past Wade, the man sitting in the back seat peered out the window. The man stared at Wade with a sullen, and desperate look on his face.

"Well, I'll be darn..." Wade muttered, watching Tyler Cummings roll by him.

The police cars continued around the oval and exited onto Elm Street, which led to the new police station over on Garden Street.

A sporty Volvo wagon followed the caravan a few car lengths back. The driver looked serious. Wade recognized him, too. Mason Walters was a Nashua lawyer who'd been in the papers and on the news in stories about several high-profile cases.

"So, that's who he hired," Wade said aloud.

How can Tyler afford a lawyer like that? Wade pondered.

Wade considered the situation, then broke for his truck. Wade always figured he had a strong hold on the company's bank accounts. But you could never be too careful, especially when your business partner was being hauled in by the police twice in the same day.

Something's gone down, Wade thought, climbing into the cab of his truck. *And I need to know what.*

CHAPTER EIGHTEEN

MASON WALTERS turned onto Elm Street and followed the caravan of police vehicles to the station. The cruisers and SUVs pulled into the police lot to the left of the building, then a few officers escorted Tyler into the station through a side door.

Mason parked in the civilian lot, located in front of the large brick building. Then he climbed out of his sport wagon and walked across the macadam towards the front doors.

Stepping through a set of shiny plate-glass double doors, he found himself standing in a lobby with a high ceiling and polished tile floors. A scent of Pine-sol floated through the space. He remembered when the station was located in a refurbished automobile dealership on the west side of town, and before that when it was housed in a musty space beneath the town hall.

Mason spotted the reception window. A young, portly police officer sat behind bulletproof glass.

Approaching the window, Mason waited a moment for the young lad to look up at him. The kid had watched Mason enter the lobby. Now, the young officer was suddenly consumed with important paperwork. Mason knew the drill: pretend you've got pressing work to do, and you'll project an image of power and importance.

The young officer finally looked up. He flashed a perfunctory smile, and it was anything but friendly. "Can I help you?" he said.

"My client was just brought in. I'd like to see him."

"And you are...?"

"Mason Walters. I'm Tyler Cummings' attorney." Mason figured the young cop knew exactly who he was there to see, but the kid was going to make him jump through every hoop.

"Please take a seat," the young officer said, pointing to a wooden bench.

"How long is it going to be?" asked Mason.

"Not sure."

Turning away, Mason walked over to the bench. It was propped against a long wall off to the side of the lobby, not too far from a door leading out back. The bench had a hard, wooden seat and a backrest to match. He figured it might be the most uncomfortable seating he'd ever seen outside of a courtroom.

"Nah," he muttered to himself.

Mason dug his hand into a pocket and fished out his cellphone. He stood near the bench, checking his messages, while waiting for someone to lead him out back.

Nothing major had developed while he'd been gone from the office.

Emergency situations often arose when he was out. It never failed. Mason could spend three days straight working at his desk in the office without a single hiccup. Then, he'd leave for court or to investigate a lead and suddenly everyone had a pressing issue. An important client's kid got arrested, a business client needed a lien filed, or a temporary restraining order. Sometimes opposing counsel would file an emergency motion, which required an immediate response.

It almost felt like a luxury being able to stay out of the office without having to put out a fire. Mason took a deep breath and finally sat down on the bench, feeling more relaxed.

He waited. And he waited, but nobody came out to greet him and accompany him to see his client.

Then, he began wondering what might be going on back there. Tyler was fairly intelligent, but he came across as quite naïve. Mason wondered if they were trying to get him to talk. Police officers could often be brazen. Even with an attorney sitting in the lobby, they might try to coax Tyler into waiving his right to counsel.

Mason ruminated on the possible discussion going down out

back: *You don't need your lawyer. You can talk to us. Maybe we can help you.* All they needed was the suspect to say okay on the record.

He grew even more worried and considered returning to the officer at the window. Then, he thought better of that approach, and decided to keep waiting, at least a little longer.

Finally, a female plainclothes officer stepped from a side door and approached him. She was a little on the shorter side, and her dirty blonde hair was swept back in a ponytail. She was dressed in black with a narrow, gray tie.

Her cold demeanor wasn't inviting. "I'm Detective Sergeant LeClair," she said.

Mason stood up. "I'm Mason Walters."

She didn't smile or offer her hand. "We know."

He wondered what case he'd handled to make them dislike him. Mason had grown up in the town. He'd worked a number of cases in Milford, but none that were out of the ordinary. Probably something that had gotten into the news and didn't sit well with some of them.

"May I see my client?" he asked.

"Follow me." She turned before he could say anything further.

LeClair used her passkey and led him into a corridor. There was a reinforced steel door at the end of the hallway, which led further into the station. A scent of ammonia wafted up from the tile flooring. They passed through the metal door into a hallway lined with interview rooms and a conference room.

Stepping into an interrogation room, she motioned for Mason to enter. He found Tyler Cummings handcuffed to the table. A uniformed officer sat in a metal chair across from him. Despite being a new police station, the room had a faint smell of urine.

Mason pulled out a chair and it squeaked on the floor. He sat beside his client.

LeClair took a seat opposite him.

"So, what's this about?" Mason said.

"We've already arrested your client for conspiracy to commit arson," LeClair said, sternly. "Now we're thinking of upping the charges to arson and felony murder."

"This all happened in Wilton," said Mason. "Why are we talking about it here in Milford?"

LeClair nodded. "The Wilton Police asked us to take the lead with this interview."

Interview? Mason thought. He doubted they had enough for an arrest.

"Officer Durham is here from Wilton," she said, indicating to the uniformed officer seated next to her. "The state police will likely get involved soon."

All murders in New Hampshire are handled by a detective bureau in the state police department. The Attorney General's Office prosecutes murder cases, rather than the County Attorney's Office or a town Police Prosecutor. Once things were turned over from the local authorities, it would be more difficult to get a decent plea deal. Mason got the feeling they wanted Tyler to sing, but he also suspected they already had a snitch.

Why do they need Tyler? That was the optimum question.

Mason shrugged. "What do you have?"

"We're not giving away the store just yet," LeClair said. "He talks, and we'll consider a favorable deal."

"I can't let a client go into this blind," Mason said, shaking his head.

"Things are moving fast on this." LeClair inhaled. "We can't promise anything."

"Can you give us a minute?" asked Mason.

LeClair and the uniformed officer locked glances, then Officer Durham nodded to her. They got up and quietly left the room, easing the door closed behind them.

Tyler looked like he was about to cry. "They think I killed someone," he said.

"Please try to hold it together. We don't have much time here."

Tyler nodded, understanding. "Okay," he said. And it came

out like a whimper.

"Look, they want to get you talking without offering anything concrete," Mason said.

"So, I shouldn't talk?" Tyler looked at him for direction.

"Ordinarily, I'd say you definitely shouldn't talk."

"But here…"

"It might be your only chance to cut a deal," Mason explained. "This matter will be turned over to the state police if there really is a death involved. The Staties tend to play hardball."

Tyler stared down at the table, unsettled.

Mason glanced around the room, waiting for the moment to pass. It was a cramped interrogation room, with concrete block walls painted tan. Even the table was small. The station was fairly new, and everything was clean. He was left with the impression of an orderly, rural town police department, which didn't typically handle big cases.

"What do we do?" Tyler finally asked.

"Depends on whether you killed anyone."

"I didn't," Tyler pled.

"What about the fire?" Mason said.

"I didn't do that, either."

"So, you're innocent. Is that what you're saying?"

"I'm saying, it's exactly like I told you from the beginning. Everything."

"Except, they seem to have found a gas can from your barn at the crime scene."

"I don't know anything about that," Tyler said.

Mason nodded. "Okay, then."

"What?"

"You talk to them. If you didn't do these things, there shouldn't be any way for them to trip you up. Hopefully, they'll offer you a deal, or divulge something to us."

"You think they'll give me a good deal?"

"Honestly?"

"Yeah."

"No. I don't."

"Why?"

"Because you can't give them anything," Mason said, shaking his head. "Heck, they're likely on a fishing expedition. I wouldn't be surprised if they think you're a patsy."

"So, should we still talk?"

"Once the Staties get involved, we won't learn anything."

Tyler sat back. "Okay, bring them in."

Mason got up and opened the door. He poked his head out. The officers were standing down the hall chatting. When LeClair looked over at him, Mason waved for them to return.

He took a seat next to Tyler and waited for the officers.

LeClair entered the room first, carrying a manilla folder. She sat across from Tyler. The uniformed officer pulled out a chair and sat down. Gear affixed to his belt clanked and rattled as he nestled into the chair. He stared coldly at Mason then he looked at Tyler.

Taking a moment, both of the police officers eyeballed the suspect. The intimidation tactic was meant to put Tyler on edge, and it seemed to be working. He squirmed in his chair.

"Why don't we get started?" Mason said.

"Sure," LeClair said, resting her hands on the folder. The contents were meant to be kept secret for now.

"What do you want to know?" Tyler said, trying to recapture some power.

The kid wasn't quite as meek or naïve as Mason had initially thought.

"We can start by your confirming a few things," LeClair said.

"Sounds fine."

"You and your business partners bought the mill from Herbert Jenkins with a note, right?" LeClair said.

Tyler nodded. "Yes."

"You also had a life insurance policy on him?" she asked, like reading from a checklist.

They figured that out too quickly, Mason thought. Now, he was certain one of the partners had already flipped. The police really didn't need Tyler if that was the case. Mason was tempted to end the discussion.

"Sure," Tyler said.

"You know he's dead," said LeClair.

"I've heard that."

"One of your gas cans was found at the mill."

Tyler shook his head. "I've never brought one there."

"We took a few latent fingerprints off the can. The state lab will confirm whether it was your gas can at the scene."

"Even if it was my can, doesn't mean I brought it there. Anyone could have—"

Mason grabbed Tyler's arm, indicating for him to shut up.

The kid looked at him and stopped talking.

"We found another gas can in your barn," LeClair continued. "Two similar cans, and likely we'll match fingerprints from the can at the scene to your prints from when you were booked this morning. That's enough to proceed forward with a straight arson charge."

"But I didn't bring the can to the mill!" Tyler protested. "Ever..." He sounded convincing.

"We've got a bigger problem," LeClair said, staring coolly at Tyler.

"Yeah?" Tyler said.

"Jenkins was found dead at the scene," she said.

"How did he die?" This from Mason.

"That's going to take a couple days," LeClair responded. "Maybe even a week. But right now, we're proceeding like he died from smoke inhalation."

Felony murder, Mason thought.

"I left before the fire," Tyler insisted.

"Doesn't necessarily matter," LeClair said. "If you agreed to a plan to burn the place for insurance money, then you brought cans of gas from your home...and poured gas all over the place to serve as an accelerant. And Herbert Jenkins died..."

"I didn't pour gas at the mill!" Tyler snapped. "None of that is true."

"If all that happened," LeClair said, calmly. "We've got you for felony murder."

"What?" Tyler asked, canting his head.

"Jenkins died because of your actions to commit arson, a felony," LeClair said, never missing a beat. "You'll go down for felony murder."

Mason leaned forward. "All right. What is it you want?"

"Look, we all know your client doesn't have a record. But Wade Garrett has been in trouble since high school. Tell us what Mr. Cummings knows and we'll consider a favorable plea deal."

"But I don't know anything," Tyler whimpered.

"That's too bad," LeClair said, coldly.

"He can't cough up evidence he doesn't have," said Mason.

"His gas can was at the scene. We know that gasoline was the accelerant. And he's just admitted to being there around the time of the fire." LeClair shrugged. "It doesn't look good for him. Now is the time to cut a deal. Tell us something. What did Wade Garrett tell you to do?"

"Like I've been saying," Tyler blurted, "I don't know anything."

LeClair stared at him for a moment, as though contemplating her next move.

Mason got the feeling the detective truly believed Tyler was caught up in an arson scheme. She'd gotten an important detail from someone. Mason also sensed that she figured there was a bigger fish to fry, someone like this Wade Garrett fellow. The case was turning out to be quite dicey.

"All right, then," LeClair said, standing up. "We'll give you some time in the cooler to think about this further."

Two officers entered the room and encroached upon Tyler. The cop from Wilton joined them.

As they worked at unshackling him from the table, LeClair motioned for Mason to clear out of the way. The chains made ominous clanks on the metal table and the tile floor. Mason got up and watched as they readied Tyler for transport to a holding cell. More chains rattling and clanging followed suit, as they wrapped Tyler's arms behind his back.

LeClair stepped closer to Tyler. She reached into her back pocket and pulled out a note card. "You have the right to remain silent…"

"What are you doing that for?" Mason said. "You've already arrested him. He's out on bail for Pete's sake."

"This time, it's for arson and felony murder."

CHAPTER NINETEEN

WADE GARRETT drove up steep roads, leading into the foothills of the Monadnock mountains.

Evening had turned from dusk into the blackness of nighttime. His headlights floated over the desolate road, shining on the roadway and reflecting off pine trees lining the rural highway. The brisk fall weather was accompanied by shorter days, much shorter days.

A heap of cash sat on the seat beside him. He didn't plan to deposit it into a bank, either.

Getaway cash, he thought. Then, he snickered.

He hadn't talked to his girlfriend Crystal about his arrest yet. Everything had gone down so quickly, from the police asking him to come by the station to his arrest and bail. Then the meeting with his lawyer and the need for money to pay a retainer. Not to mention the quickie with Lexi.

Crystal had called and texted him, asking if he was okay. Wade didn't know how to broach the subject, so he hadn't called her back. He'd just responded with text messages, saying he was fine, and they could talk about it later. He preferred to have the discussion in private and not over a phone call that could possibly be tapped. Besides, he didn't particularly trust her. She could have set him up.

After seeing Tyler in the back of a squad car, Wade had booked it over to the bank and withdrawn money from the business savings and checking accounts. He left a little in the checking account to cover some payments that were still being processed. He hadn't taken time to tally it all up. Some checks might bounce, but he was more concerned with having it all to himself.

"Screw Tyler and Scott Bancroft," he muttered, while country music played on the radio.

Wade had left the bank and drove straight to the oval and parked. He stopped by his lawyer's office and paid the retainer. Kyle Wentworth hadn't batted an eye when Wade plopped twenty-five thousand in cash on the desk.

Lawyers don't care where money comes from, as long as it's green. Wade laughed.

His truck crested a hill, and he entered the town of Lyndeborough.

Turning off the main road that led into town, Wade climbed higher then banged a right where the road leveled off. He barreled down a long gravel driveway, lined with evergreens. Eventually, the gravel transitioned to pavement and the driveway ahead of him widened.

A large house loomed before him with outside lighting that illuminated the exterior. The silhouette of the enormous dwelling was outlined against a dark backdrop. Occasional windows in the new house were lit up by interior lights. The house looked quaint, peaceful. During the day, you could see mountain peaks in the distance.

Wade hit the button for a garage door opener, then he pulled the truck into the bay of a three-car garage. He parked next to a Cadillac Escalade. It was the only one left from the four vehicles he'd leased for the mill owners. When revenue contracted, he'd let the leases expire on them, except for Crystal's car. He'd extended the lease on her car and paid handsome extension fees. Now, he regretted having done that for her. *Less getaway cash.*

He climbed out of the cab and immediately felt frigid air. Stepping to a door leading into the house, he hit a button on the wall and the overhead door slowly eased closed.

Wade entered the house. The place was quiet, and he could barely make out the buzz from a television in the family room. It was warm inside. He slipped out of his trucker's jacket, then hung it on a coatrack in the hallway.

The polished plank floors creaked under his boots as he walked into the kitchen. A hint of diced onions hung in the air.

The kitchen was large with exposed overhead beams and pine cabinets lining two walls. The woodwork was shellacked and sparkled even in the dim lighting. Most of the walls were bare, despite the couple having lived in the house for over a year. A new farmer's table and chairs were located near a bay window that overlooked the backyard.

The kitchen had shiny black appliances and a smooth electric cooktop.

He moved further into the room and smelled the aroma of dinner.

A large pot simmered on the stove, and a scent of beef stew wafted through the room. Wade hadn't eaten since breakfast, and his stomach turned from the soup's aroma, reminding him of his hunger.

"Crystal," he softly called out. He planned to treat this delicately. He might need her.

"I'm in here," she shouted from the family room.

Wade stepped into a short hallway and entered the massive gathering room with a vaulted ceiling. It had exposed beams and a wall was lined with a large bookcase. Most of the cubbies were empty. Knickknacks that Crystal had picked up over the years were set on a few of the shelves. The woodwork shimmered in the evening light.

He found her seated on a plush, brown leather sofa. Crystal's feet were on the cushion with her knees tucked under her chin. She held a can of Coors Light in her hand.

Wade could go for a yellow jacket about now.

"How you doing?" he said, tenderly. And he meant it.

"You've been on the evening news," she said sadly. "All the highlights were about you. They had shots of you coming and going from the police station."

"Anybody else?" He was wondering if Bancroft was seen there.

"Nope. Just you," Crystal said. "At least that's all I saw."

Daddy probably arranged for Bancroft to slip in and out a side door, he concluded.

Wade walked over to the sofa and plopped down next to her. Suddenly, he wasn't hungry anymore. His stomach turned and cramped up; his pulse raced from anxiety. Glancing at the television, he waited in dismay for the news story to come back on.

"You hate to see something like this," Crystal said. "But somehow you can't help but watch."

Wade nodded. That was exactly how he felt.

"Care for a sip of my beer?" she said.

"Sure."

She handed over the beer, and he took a long swig. "That's damn good," he said, offering the can back to her.

"You can have it," she said, "Probably need it more than me."

"So, what are they saying?" he asked.

"You know the news. They don't ever say a whole lot." Crystal shrugged. "They showed some shots with a reporter and the burnt mill in the background. And they kept showing you coming out of the police station. All they said was three men were suspected of arson and that a body was found at the mill. The death was being investigated."

"The death was being investigated," Wade mumbled. *That don't mean murder.*

"Wade," she said softly. "You shouldn't get your hopes up."

He looked at her. "What's that supposed to mean?"

"It means it usually takes a couple of days for a medical examiner to determine the cause of death in situations like this."

All the air left the room. Wade found it hard to breathe.

"They're going to tie that body to the fire," she said. "You can bet your life on it."

"You really think so?" he asked.

"Certainly." And she sounded sure.

Wade sat back and guzzled the rest of the beer. He crushed the can, then he set it on the coffee table. It wobbled. Then, the beer can fell over with a faint metallic clang.

He shook his head, dejected. "You sure about this?"

"That's what I expect," she said, nodding.

Wade cringed. Then, he clenched his jaw tight, feeling the molars grind against each other. He didn't like where this was headed, and he began to worry about Crystal cutting loose. She might even turn against him, if she hadn't done so already. She'd left a boyfriend in a jam before he'd met her.

"Are we going to lose the house," Crystal said after a moment.

"I'm not sure," he said, trying to sound honest with some level of reassurance. Hope.

"Thought we'd get married. Then eventually have kids running around this place," she said. "I figured we'd pay off the mortgage and grow old here."

"Look, we're not necessarily going to lose the house."

"How can you say that?" she griped. "We've lost the mill and we can't pay the mortgage with you in prison."

"There's insurance money," he pled.

"Fat chance of them paying out... now that you've been arrested." Her tone had turned cold, bitter. "Insurance companies aren't stupid, you know."

"Sure. I know that."

"Well, I'm not going back to stripping," Crystal said.

Her comment caught him off guard. It had been so long since he'd even thought about what she was doing when they'd met. Seemed like a lifetime ago. He was managing a mill in Denver and would unwind at a topless bar on the edge of town. Crystal took it all off for the right price, but she swore that she'd never sold her body. He believed her, too.

"I'm not going to jail," Wade snapped. "I didn't torch that place. And I certainly didn't kill anyone."

Crystal sat there staring at him with a surprised look on her face. He could see that she wanted to believe him. But there was a hint of doubt in her eyes.

CHAPTER TWENTY

MASON pulled out of the police station parking lot questioning whether he should have let Tyler speak with them. The result was dismal; his client was locked in a holding cell, and the police hadn't revealed anything new.

The cops had gotten information without coughing up a darn thing, Mason thought.

He drove along Route 101A and headed out of town. Mason crossed the Amherst town line and came to a stop at a traffic light. He fished his cellphone out of a coat pocket and managed to pull up his contacts before the light turned green.

Mason banged a right onto rural highway 122 and headed towards the sleepy town of Hollis.

A moment later, he had Ray Jefferson on the line. Ray was a retired police detective who ran a private investigation firm.

"I need a little help here," Mason said.

"Yeah. I've seen your case on the news," Ray said.

"This one has some tricky angles. We're going to need to get a jump on it."

"What do you need?" asked Ray.

"A copy of the police report. I need it *before* the probable cause hearing."

There was a pause before Ray responded. "That could be a little tricky. Cops in the small departments aren't as keen to turn things over. Not in this state."

"I figured that," Mason said. "But if we do get a report, it's less likely to be a stacked deck."

"True," Ray said. "However, small town cops might just

shortchange you."

Mason considered the comment. They were talking about the practices of police departments in how they deal with private investigators and turning over information.

Sometimes, a cop will slip a private investigator a copy of a police report as a favor or for a payment. Other times, an officer reports the request to his superiors, and they use the situation as an opportunity to throw a defense attorney off the trail. They stack the deck by putting in a piece of false evidence, and they occasionally shortchange you by removing certain items from the report, such as a key witness statement or a forensics report.

"Just do the best you can," Mason finally said. "I'll take whatever they provide to you with a grain of salt."

"Will do. Skepticism is the best approach."

"Thanks for helping with this."

"No problem."

Mason ended the call and focused on the dark country road ahead, wondering if Jenkins had died from the fire, natural causes, or whether somebody had murdered the old man.

CHAPTER
TWENTY-ONE

CROSSING over the Hollis town line, Mason traveled down a rural highway listening to a public radio station. News about the economy dominated the broadcast and his arson case never got any airtime.

Eventually, he turned onto South Merrimack Road then veered onto Farley Road.

The lonesome stretch of pavement was dark, but a familiar dip in the roadway alerted him to slow. Mason turned left onto a dirt driveway, which headed into the back of a six-acre lot.

His Volvo sports wagon jostled over potholes that he never got around to filling.

The driveway ran past a four-hundred-year-old antique cape style house, then circled around in front of a three-stall carriage shed. His tires crunched over gravel as he rolled up to it. A Ford F-250 was parked beside the shed. He used the truck for plowing the long driveway and pulling his boat. A John Deere tractor occupied the first stall, along with his Mako skiff that sat on a boat trailer. His wife's Volvo SUV took up the last bay.

Mason rolled into the middle slot and parked his car. Climbing out of the small wagon, he felt drained from the excitement of the day. Things had taken a drastic turn. Within a brief time, his new case had evolved from a weak conspiracy to commit arson charge to straight arson and felony murder. Mason wondered if the detective had acted rashly. They couldn't have had the medical examiner's findings this soon.

Mason opened the back door of the wagon and snagged his knapsack. He considered retrieving his fishing gear from the way back. "Nah," he said aloud, waving a hand at it. *I'll just end up hauling it out here again in a few days.*

He walked over to the house and entered through a side door, stepping into a mudroom. Then he trundled over the antique plank floors, worn from the ages, trying to find his way in the dark. Mason fished around for a light switch and found purchase. Turning on the hall light, he then dropped the backpack on the floor and removed his ballcap. He shoved the hat into a cubby, then he slid out of his waxed jacket and hung the coat on a peg.

Kicking off his short Wellies, he then opened a door leading into a gourmet kitchen. His wool socks kept his feet warm as he started across the cool tile floor.

A pattering of feet clicked across the ceramic tile floor. Their dog had come to greet him, wiggling its body as it approached.

"Hey, Benny," Mason said, reaching down to pet the dog.

The dog wagged its tail. A Griffon pointer and black Labrador retriever mix, the dog had a black head and upper torso, with a white body and paws that were covered in black spots. Benny was named after Fort Bennington, where Mason had attended boot camp and infantry school.

"How you doing?" Mason said, giving the dog another pat.

The kitchen was part of an addition, which they had a local architect design.

Counters ran along two walls in a classic L-shaped arrangement, and there was an island in the center with stools. The cabinets were white, and the countertops were made from a black, polished soapstone. The island had a marble countertop. Two sets of sliding glass doors opened to a large brick patio area on the back of the house. A rustic kitchen table and chairs was situated in a nook, close to the patio doors. A couple place settings were already spread out on the table.

The gourmet kitchen was complemented with stainless

steel, professional-grade Viking appliances. A hanging pot rack dangled from the ceiling over an island, loaded with pots and pans, which had seen a lot of use. Various utensils were also hung on the rack. The range and exhaust hood were soiled from years of cooking and hasty cleanup efforts.

Mason smelled the aroma of homemade spaghetti sauce. He glanced at the range and noticed a pot simmering on the gas cooktop.

He looked around for his wife. The addition included an adjacent family room, but she wasn't there. Mason stepped into a hallway and saw light stemming from the front living room. Making his way towards the parlor, he listened to see if his wife was watching the news. But the only sound he heard was his footsteps treading over the old plank floors, and the pattering of paws as Benny trailed behind him.

Entering the living room, he found her seated on a Chippendale sofa reading a book. Behind her was a wall of built-in bookcases, made from pine boards with wainscoting for the backboards. The bookcases were painted white and filled with British and American literature. A few shelves housed Mason's non-fiction books on fly fishing and history, while the rest mainly housed their literary tomes. Some of the books were duplicates from courses they'd taken together in college: Chaucer, Milton, and Shakespeare.

"There you are," he said, standing on a braided rug in front of a large fireplace.

Amelia looked up at him and slid her reading glasses down her nose.

"Looks like you've made dinner," Mason said.

"I've gotten a start on the sauce. But I haven't made the pasta."

"Well, I would have made the sauce if you'd waited for me to get home."

"You've had a hard enough day," Amelia said.

"So, you've heard about it."

"Yes, I have," Amelia said, rising. "One can always count on the entire teaching staff to keep me apprised of your activities. They pick these things up on social media, reading stories on their phones between classes."

Amelia was the principal of a local high school. Prior to moving into administration, she had taught English for many years. She had worked full-time teaching, and raised two daughters, while earning her doctorate in education. Amelia had commuted to Boston University in order to obtain the coveted Ed.D credential.

"I didn't mean for it to bother you," Mason said.

"No bother," she replied, setting her book down on a tea table.

"Can't be easy hearing news about crimes from your teachers." Mason shrugged.

"Well, I'm used to it," she said, walking towards him. Amelia had shoulder-length black hair, peppered with gray strands, which bobbed when she walked. She didn't have any plans of coloring her hair.

"Your gait is off a bit," he said.

"Just a sore hip from running," Amelia said, waving him off.

Mason leaned forward and gave her a peck on the cheek.

They turned and headed into the kitchen, with Benny trotting after them. It was a well-used room, with prints of landscapes hanging on the walls and family photographs stuck to the refrigerator with magnets. Each magnet featured one of their jaunts: hiking in New Hampshire and Vermont, fishing in Montana and Alaska, and downhill skiing around New England.

Amelia stood behind the island and reached for a pot from the hanging rack.

"I could cook the spaghetti," Mason offered.

"You tend to do all the cooking on pasta night," Amelia said. "I don't mind the change up. Why don't you go fetch us a bottle of wine?"

"Sure thing."

Mason opened the door leading into the cellar, flipped a light switch, and headed down a steep set of rickety stairs.

The cellar was more of a glorified crawlspace than a basement. It was an eight by ten area surrounded by large granite blocks and fieldstones, with a dirt floor. The ceiling was low enough that Mason had to duck under the beams. A wine rack ran along the wall opposite the furnace.

He considered the various options, finally settling on an Italian red. It was one he'd been holding on to for a few years. Mason selected the bottle of Barolo then plodded upstairs.

Amelia stood at the island preparing dinner, and Benny was snug in his bed tucked in a corner of the room.

Mason walked over to the cupboard and grabbed two wine glasses. Then he used a waiter's corkscrew to open the bottle. Pouring two glasses, he sniffed the bouquet and took a sip. "Pretty good," he said, sliding a glass over to Amelia.

She took a sip and smiled. "Delicious."

"Might not be much left over after dinner," Mason said, chuckling.

Amelia glanced at the bottle. "Barolo. I thought this tasted too good. What's the occasion?"

"None." Mason shrugged. "Just thought with a big case, I won't get much time to indulge in the coming months."

"You mean...with a fat retainer check, you could afford to satiate with extravagant wine."

"Something like that," he admitted, cracking a wan smile, feeling slightly chagrined.

Mason walked over and opened a cabinet they used for storing bread. He pulled out a loaf of French bread and placed it on the island. Tearing off a piece, he took a bite and washed it down with wine. "That hits the spot," he said.

"Grab a couple plates," Amelia said, pouring the spaghetti into a strainer in the sink.

Mason did as he was told. Soon, they were settled at the table with a heap of pasta on their plates. He hadn't realized how hungry he'd gotten from not eating for several hours.

They ate quietly for a bit.

When the food eventually settled his stomach, Mason sat

back in his chair and took a long sip of wine. He finished off the glass. Then, he partially refilled it. "Do you want any more?" he asked, indicating to the bottle.

Amelia shook her head. "I've got a little work to do tonight."

"Suit yourself," Mason said, then he poured a little more wine into his glass.

"Can you tell me what this case is about?" she asked.

"Why don't we start by talking about your day?" Mason said.

Amelia rolled her eyes. "I'm afraid that my day was pretty much like many others, with the exception that my husband got himself involved in the most publicized criminal matter in the Souhegan Valley."

Mason was taken aback. "Well, I figured it went something like that."

"You wouldn't know what that is like, unless you've experience it."

"I couldn't agree more," he said, raising his glass in a mock toast.

"Your sentiments are appreciated," Amelia said after a moment. "So, are you able to talk about this new case?"

"Afraid that I don't know enough to intelligently converse on the subject."

"If you did know more, would you tell me?" she asked.

Mason ruminated over her question. It came up all the time. His work was subject to attorney/client privilege. During his entire career, he'd never revealed the content of a client's discussions with her. He often danced around strategic considerations, which were protected as well. The best practice was to leave his work at the office.

Most of the time, that's what she preferred. However, he was getting the distinct impression that for some reason, she wanted to know more about this particular case.

"What gives?" he finally asked.

"I'm not exactly sure what you mean," she said.

"You know we don't talk about cases, but you seem to want to discuss this one," Mason said. "I'm curious what piqued your interest?"

Amelia sat back considering the question. "This one is different."

"How so?" And he really wanted to know.

"You've defended people who committed crimes," she said, taking a sip of wine, as though gathering more thought. "There have been murder cases. People committed horrific acts that resulted in the death of another..."

"And?"

"Those were all done in the heat of the moment."

"We don't know exactly what happened in this case yet," Mason reasoned.

"That's true," Amelia said, nodding.

"But you've heard things that are starting to shape your opinion about it?"

Amelia nodded. "Yes."

"What are they?" he said.

He was asking more from an attorney's standpoint than a husband's interest. Mason wondered how the case was shaping up from a public viewpoint. Amelia's perspective could be representative of the eventual jury pool who might be called to serve at trial.

"You have a few businessmen who apparently got into dire financial troubles," she said.

"Okay."

"They owed money to this old gentleman," she continued. "Authorities say the mill fire was caused by arson. The same time the place caught fire, the old man died there. Well, that's too much to be a coincidence."

Mason thought about her summary. It was damn good.

"You can see how my teachers might perceive this," Amelia added.

"Certainly," Mason said. "This can't be easy for you."

"You, either," she said, and flashed a grin.

"Touché," he replied and chuckled.

"So, what can I tell my people?" Amelia said after a moment.

"Afraid I can't say much." Mason shrugged. "My client is fairly naïve. When he eventually gets featured in the press, one would expect him to come across much differently from this Wade Garrett fellow."

"Can't believe I'm saying this," she replied, "but I am looking forward to the press getting ahold of your client."

"Just like ripping a band-aid off, sometimes it's better to do it quickly," Mason said.

***

THEY spent the rest of the meal talking about their two daughters, who were both away at college.

Their older daughter was studying psychology at the University of Vermont, and the younger daughter was studying English as part of a pre-law program at Auburn University. Academics for the younger daughter were occasionally interrupted by equestrian events. Mason wondered if she'd ever return to New Hampshire to join his law practice.

After they finished dinner, Mason and Amelia cleared the table.

He loaded the dishwasher, and he straightened things up. Benny kept to his side, waiting for any scraps that happen to fall on the floor.

"Surprisingly, we didn't drink all the wine," Mason said, corking the bottle.

"What's surprising is that *you* didn't drink more."

They both laughed. Then, he opened a refrigerator door and put the wine bottle in a door bin, fiddling with bottles to wedge it in place. Closing the door, he found Amelia standing at the island with her hands placed on the counter.

"Well, that's everything," she said.

"Do you want to watch a show on Brit Box?" he asked, suspecting he knew the answer.

"I'd like to," Amelia said. "But I have some work to finish up."

"Things you didn't get to during the day?"

"Pretty much."

"I'll get out of your hair then."

"You could still watch something. Just not one of my favorite programs."

"No. Think I'll go putter around."

"Okay," Amelia said, then she headed for the formal living room.

Mason figured she'd work at her antique secretary desk, which had a hutch on the top with glass doors and shelves for smaller books. A pocket-sized collection of Shakespeare and a few others were situated inside the hutch. Later, he'd likely find her seated there with the desk-lid pulled open and a laptop nestled on it.

He walked into the hallway and fetched his waxed jacket and ballcap. Then, he slid on his short Wellies, grabbed the knapsack, and headed for a side door, leading to a brick walkway off the back of the house. Benny trucked after him.

"No. You stay with Mum," he said to the dog.

Benny slowly wagged his tail and looked sadly into Mason's eyes.

"You really want to go out?" Mason said, encouragingly.

The dog's eyes lit up. Benny lifted his head and his tail whapped rapidly back and forth.

"Okay, then." Mason patted the dog. Then, he opened the door and cool air whipped inside. Benny bolted past him and ran into the snow-covered yard.

Stepping outside, a frigid wind blew hard and turned Mason's cheeks raw.

Mason headed over the walkway towards an outbuilding, while Benny sniffed around the grass near a stone wall. Beyond the wall was a paddock and a six-stall horse barn. The barn stood empty with their younger daughter's sport horse away with her at college.

Several years beforehand, Mason and Amelia had converted an old cooper's shed on the property into a makeshift office. He stepped inside the outbuilding and called for the dog. Benny trotted over and scampered into the shed.

Mason closed the door, shutting out the cold. The shed smelled musty. Flipping on an overhead light, it was frigid enough inside the shed for him to see his breath. Mason busied himself with firing up the pellet stove, located in a corner of the shed. Within a few minutes, warmth radiated through the small outbuilding. Benny nestled on the floor beside the stove, balled up with his paws tucked in close.

The shed was about sixteen feet long and nine feet wide. Mason had installed insulation in the rough framed walls, then finished the interior with knotty pine paneling. Prints of various trout species hung on the walls.

A couple of windows were located on the back of the shed, looking out into the woods. During the day, he caught occasional glimpses of a shimmering brook that ran behind the property. Fishing rod racks and storage cabinets were affixed to the back wall above the windows. The racks were loaded with fly fishing rods, and his gear hung from pegs mounted in the back wall. Another window was situated on the front of the outbuilding not far from the door. A small, oak paneled desk was pressed against the wall beneath the lone window.

Mason's fly-tying vise with wooden base was located on the desk.

Taking a seat at the desk, he gently pushed the fly-tying workstation aside. He wriggled his laptop from a compartment in the backpack and set it on the desk. He turned it on. While the machine started up, he reached into the deep drawer of the desk and pulled out a bottle of Booker's small batch bourbon. He fished out an old-fashioned glass and poured a finger of bourbon into the glass.

He took a sip and it burned. Mason leaned over and yanked the door to his mini-fridge open. Grabbing a few ice cubes, he deposited them into the drink. Then, he added a tick more bourbon, swirled the cubes around, and took another sip.

Much better, he thought.

Clicking the mouse on various prompts, he quickly had the

screen up with the inbox to his firm email account opened. There were a few emails from clients, along with various inquiries from vendors trying to get his business. Amid the unread emails, he spotted the one he was searching for. Mason clicked on the message from Ray Jefferson.

Even as he opened the email, Mason noticed that it was sent with an attachment.

The police report! Jefferson had come through and rather quickly.

Mason opened the document. He sipped bourbon and read through it, skimming over the content. It was his practice to undertake a cursory review of a document like this. He'd take a mental note of the parts that comprised the report, then he would go back and review each section in detail. With a police report, he looked to see what statements they had obtained, which officers had contributed to the report, and whether any forensic results were included with the document.

This was clearly a preliminary report. It hadn't even been finalized. Most police reports require a supervisor to approve and sign the final version of a report. No one had signed off on this report, so it was still subject to revision and supplementation.

He carefully read over the section related to Herbert Jenkins.

Mason smiled. "The devil is in the details," he muttered.

CHAPTER TWENTY-TWO

WADE GARRETT knew he had to make nice with Crystal to keep her on his side. Someone had already turned against him, and he couldn't afford to have another person with knowledge of his business to flip for the police.

He'd been around long enough to know that many cases weren't solved through careful police investigations into the evidence. Arrests often hinged on people ratting out their partners in crime. If people just kept their mouths shut, the police wouldn't have the proof necessary to support a conviction.

After dinner, he'd taken a shower to rinse off any scent of Lexi. Wade had explained the shower to Crystal by saying he needed to get the stink of the jail off him. But he hadn't even spent a second in a jail cell. She didn't know that, though.

Later, he fetched her a beer, got her loose, then he wooed her with flattery. They'd wound up in bed. She lay naked under the covers beside him, while he stared up at the ceiling. Wade was too keyed up to sleep. He wondered what Tyler had said to the police. Then he considered whether Scott Bancroft had ratted them out. His thoughts went further into speculating whether they had both flipped on him.

Maybe Crystal had ratted me out, or Lexi? He couldn't be certain.

Wade's mind turned to the getaway money sitting on the

seat of his pickup truck. He hadn't brought it inside. And he never mentioned withdrawing the money to Crystal. Something caused him to hold back on telling her everything.

Heck, she could be working for the police right now, he thought. *Stupid bitch.*

Leaning over, he checked to see if she was awake. Crystal was still out like a light.

Wade slid out of bed and wriggled into his jeans. Then he wriggled into a T-shirt and pulled on a pair of socks. He tiptoed downstairs and eased the door leading to the garage open. Walking across the frigid cement floor, he listened to make sure Crystal hadn't woken up and treaded down the stairs after him.

The house was eerily quiet.

Opening the door to the truck, he stretched over the seat and grabbed the bag full of money. He began to close the truck door, but he decided to wait until after he'd hidden the money. The sound might stir Crystal awake.

Wade scanned the garage and came up empty. The house was too new. It wasn't packed with extraneous items from years of living in the same place. He didn't have a lot of options. Putting the money anywhere inside the house was risky. Crystal didn't go in the garage much, but she was bound to dig into every closet or cubby in the house.

He looked over at the workbench and toolboxes.

A tool cabinet with a wooden top caught his attention. It was chock-full of clunky items: a reciprocating saw, sanding machines, and orange extension cords.

That's it, he thought.

Wade walked over and snagged a yellow extension cord off the workbench. He often used it for outdoor work, like the electric weedwhacker. It wouldn't be needed this time of year. Unzipping the gym bag, he shoved the cord inside. The cord did a nice job of covering the money.

Then, he opened the steel cabinet, pulled out a bunch of items, and placed the bag in the back of cabinet on the bottom shelf. He carefully replaced everything in front of the bag stuffed with money, arranging things so it wasn't noticeable.

He closed the cabinet doors.

Wade inhaled. Then, he stood up, and he walked back over to the driver's side door of the truck. Lightly pressing the door into place, he waited for resistance. Then he gave the door a gentle shove and it clicked closed without echoing into the house. It was a trick he'd learned as a kid when he went woodchuck hunting with his father.

His father would drive around with a hunting rifle in the trunk. If his dad saw a woodchuck in a field, he'd slow the car to the soft shoulder and roll to a stop. Then he'd get out and ease the driver's door closed to avoid scaring the woodchuck away. His father would pop the trunk lid and slide the rifle out of its case. Then he would set up on the hood of the car and take a shot at the unsuspecting animal. Most of the time, it was a hit. And his father would come back around to the rear of the car with a big grin on his face, as he slid the rifle into its case.

This memory ran through Wade's mind in the flick of a moment, and it reminded him that he'd stalked unsuspecting prey his entire life.

He headed back into the house, cutting off the light behind him.

Wade walked into the kitchen and found Crystal standing near the island wearing a nightshirt.

"Hey," he said, trying to sound casual.

"What were you doing?" she said, tilting her head skeptically.

"I couldn't sleep," Wade said. "Thought I heard something, so I came down to check it out. Didn't find anything…"

Crystal furrowed her brow and looked at him suspiciously. She clearly didn't believe him. But she didn't say anything further.

Wade felt relieved that she didn't make him explain further.

She poured herself a glass of water from the tap, took a long sip, then she turned and, without saying another word, headed upstairs. The tension hung so heavy in the air, you could cut it with a knife.

CHAPTER TWENTY-THREE

THE NEXT WEEK, Mason pulled up to the Milford District Court and found the parking lot packed with cars and a couple of news vans.

The courthouse was a two-and-one-half-story brick building with a mansard roof that housed dormers and a gable over the front entrance. It was topped by a belfry with a pyramidal roof, which jutted into the skyline. Perched on a slight hill, the courthouse projected a menacing image of the legal system. A dusting of snow and early morning mist served to amplify the imposing tableau of the structure.

Previously, the district court had been located on an upper floor of the town hall, with large windows overlooking Union Square. The current location was the result of a historical renovation project, where the state had converted an 1800's schoolhouse into a District Court. A large, paved parking area was situated on the righthand side of the courthouse. The parking area was shared with the local Division of Motor Vehicles office, which was located in a brand-new one-story building with large, plate-glass windows.

Mason squeezed his sports wagon into a tight spot and climbed out of the car, hoping the commotion wasn't about his case.

Perhaps all the cars were there for the DMV, he thought. But he knew better.

He wore a gray Brooks Brothers suit, with a white dress shirt and a green and navy striped rep tie. Mason wore a 1st Infantry Division lapel pin, as a reminder of his service and unassailable integrity.

Carrying a black leather briefcase, he hoofed it towards the granite front steps.

A reporter popped out from behind a van and stepped into his path. She held a microphone and a cameraman followed her. "You're Mason Walters?" the reporter asked.

"Afraid I don't have time," Mason said. He wanted to speak with his client before the arraignment. Mason had gotten Tyler released on bail and planned to meet him before court got underway.

"This would only take a minute."

"I don't have a minute," Mason said, shaking his head.

"Please, sir," she said. "Just a moment."

He pointed at the courthouse. "I really have to run," Mason said, rushing off.

After he moved past the reporting crew, he picked up the pace to a trot. The leather heels of his black dress shoes smacked the macadam as he headed for the front doors.

"Catch that," the reporter said to her cameraman.

Mason heard the sound of the camera man's feet shuffle. Then the reporter mumbled something inaudible.

Slowing to a brisk walk, Mason wanted to avoid looking frantic on camera.

He finally reached the front steps and ascended them quickly. Mason took a deep breath, then he opened one of the double doors and stepped inside.

Entering the courthouse, he walked up to security and found a slow-moving line to get through. A court officer saw him and waved for Mason to skip the metal detector. Carl was a burly security guard, with broad shoulders and a potbelly that stretched out his uniform.

"Thanks," Mason said as he passed by.

"Figured you were all *fired up* to get to court on this one," Carl said, chuckling.

"You'd be correct," Mason replied.

It was only after he walked a little further that Carl's comment registered. *Fired up,* Mason thought. *It's an arson case. What a smart-ass.*

Mason found the lobby jampacked. People lingered around with glum faces. This wasn't just a bunch of courthouse gadflies here to see his case. It was a Monday morning arraignment day following various arrests over the weekend: drunk driving, possession of marijuana over the legal limit, possession of prescription drugs, drunk and disorderly... you name it. He'd seen it all before.

An experienced police officer or police prosecutor would eventually address the crowd and instruct them to line up in front of a conference room. Then the lead cop would meet with each defendant, one at a time, plea bargaining their crimes to whittle down the caseload. They'd go in front of the judge and plead guilty to the reduced sentence, pay a fine, and go on their way. Many would handle their charges expeditiously without realizing they were creating a criminal record, even when some of them had legitimate defenses. Mason had seen many people admit to a crime that would have been dismissed had they hired a good lawyer.

Mason checked the board and found that his case was assigned to Courtroom One.

Courthouse offices for the public were located on the first floor: the clerk's office, a parole officer's office, and various rooms packed with filing cabinets.

He took the staircase to the second level and came to a wide landing. Courtroom One was located on the right side of the building and Courtroom Two was on the left. Mason headed to the room on the right. An oak bench was perched against the wall. A few people stood outside the courtroom doors, and a lawyer sat on the bench with his briefcase snug next to him, like cuddling a stray cat.

Mason checked the doors and found them locked, as he

suspected. They didn't like to open the courtrooms until everyone was finished with the plea bargain line.

Soon, people came upstairs and spread out on the landing and in front of the courtrooms. They came up in dribs and drabs at first, then a steady line of people filtered onto the second floor. Several people used the elevator. They unloaded and trundled around trying to figure out where to go.

Scanning the place for his client, Mason spotted Tyler standing by a window on the other side of the floor near Courtroom Two. *This kid is so naïve,* Mason thought. *Couldn't even find his way to the correct courtroom.*

Mason headed over to chat with his client.

Tyler didn't notice him until Mason was a couple feet away. The kid seemed glued to the window, watching the reporters outside.

"How you holding up?" Mason said.

"Didn't sleep last night," Tyler said, turning to face Mason.

Mason paused for a moment before responding. "Afraid that's to be expected..."

"They're probably out there telling people I'm a murderer," Tyler said, motioning a thumb towards the window.

"You can count on the press to sensationalize this."

"Sure," Tyler said, mumbling. He had sad eyes.

"Listen," Mason said. "We're going to have to report to the courtroom momentarily. These matters are typically handled a certain way. But I'm thinking of approaching this differently."

"How come?" Tyler said, sounding worried.

"Just trust me. I have a plan."

CHAPTER TWENTY-FOUR

A BAILIFF stepped from the courtroom and pushed the double doors open, pressing a doorstopper in place on each door with a push of his patent leather shoe.

"Court's open!" the bailiff called out.

"Let's go," Mason said to Tyler, gently tugging the kid's arm.

Tyler walked sheepishly along, like a lamb heading to slaughter.

Entering the courtroom, Mason and Tyler followed a throng of people filing inside for their various matters. The cattle call suggested the judge anticipated Tyler's matter to unfold in the usual course.

The renovation of the old school building into a courthouse had converted the space into a pristine tower of justice. Light maple wood comprised the judge's bench, witness stand, and jury box. A new dark green carpet ran across the floor; and, the walls were painted in a light green, with an occasional offset of hunter green. The counsel tables were a lightly finished oak, and the chairs were turn of the century style oak, except they had padded seats. The pews in the gallery were also a lightly finished oak.

As people took seats in the gallery, a few members of the press squeezed in beside them. Public defenders pushed the gate open and sat in chairs on the other side of the rail, which was comprised of wrought-iron bars forged into decorative patterns and capped with an oak top-piece. The lawyers mingled and talked chummy to each other about their weekends. Most ran private practices where they entered into contracts with the state to handle overflow cases and conflicts the Public Defender's Office couldn't accept.

Mason found a spot in the first pew and took a seat next to his client.

Tyler nudged him. "That's Wade Garrett," Tyler said, pointing.

"Hmm," Mason muttered, noting the man in the trucker jacket was represented by Kyle Wentworth, a well-connected and rather smooth-talking lawyer.

A moment later, Detective Sergeant LeClair and Officer Durham entered the room. They were followed by a burly prosecutor with a balding pate. A slick looking man in a flashy suit trailed behind them. The slick man was accompanied by an older attorney with a gray beard. The older man wore a wool suit that hung loose on his boney frame, and he had a receding hairline with pepper gray hair, pulled into a short ponytail.

Mason recognized the lawyer immediately; Samuel Makinson.

Sam Makinson was the most well-known criminal defense attorney in the state. He operated out of an office in Manchester, but he had satellite offices in each region. Makinson came to fame by handling a couple of high-profile cases, including one or two that had attracted national media attention.

Makinson caught Mason's eye and nodded as he walked down the aisle.

Tyler elbowed Mason and pointed at the slick man. "That's —"

"Scott Bancroft," Mason said, finishing the comment.

"How did you know?" Tyler asked.

"Because he's with a notorious criminal defense lawyer," Mason replied, while watching the infamous lawyer and his client making their way through the gate.

The duo sat down in chairs nestled against the rail, directly behind the prosecutor's table. Such a move put an end to the question of whether someone had flipped. Mason didn't particularly care for the turn of events. He watched Bancroft seated among the cadre of police and prosecution, smiling and carrying on like he didn't have a care in the world.

Probably pled out for a misdemeanor with no jail time, Mason thought. *This won't affect his life in the least.*

***

WADE GARRETT sat beside his lawyer and watched Bancroft grinning and acting happier than a pig in shit.

Wade didn't need his lawyer to tell him what was going on. The bastard had flipped.

"Looks like Scott Bancroft has gotten chummy with the police," Kyle said, nudging him and pointing to the group hunkered around the prosecutor.

"Who's that with him?" asked Wade.

"Sam Makinson," Kyle said. "The most well-known criminal defense lawyer in the state."

"Yeah. I've heard of him."

Wade couldn't believe what he was seeing right in the courtroom. Such an open alignment of a criminal defendant with the police and prosecution seemed to him like a flagrant conflict of interest. He figured they didn't care about fairness. Heck, they probably didn't care about the truth.

"He's pretty good," Kyle said after a moment.

"I figured as much," Wade replied.

"Expensive."

"I've heard that, too."

"Bancroft's old man probably paid for it," Kyle said.

"No doubt," Wade added. "Why would a guy hire a big shot lawyer, then go and turn around and accept a plea?"

"Because a good lawyer like Makinson gets the sweet deals."

Kyle's words hung in the air like the putrid stench of a roadkill. Scanning the room, Wade spotted Tyler sitting next to the lawyer from Nashua. The kid looked nervous.

Probably has flipped, Wade thought. *Chickenshit.*

Then, he glanced over at Bancroft and the slick salesman caught him looking over. Bancroft flashed a smug grin and nodded to him. Young Bancroft and his rich father likely had all the guns pointed at Wade. Even the police and prosecutor didn't seem concerned; it was like this was going to be an easy case to them. Open and shut. A slam dunk.

"Arraignments are just a formality," Kyle said, as if reading his mind.

"Might be," Wade said. "But the other side doesn't look worried at all."

"We'll have to see how things play out," Kyle said, with a reassuring tone.

The comment didn't make Wade feel any better. He knew where he stood, and it wasn't good. Something had to give, or he'd be going away for a very long time.

CHAPTER
TWENTY-FIVE

THE JUDGE stepped through a door in the back of the courtroom, and a portly bailiff instructed everyone to rise. Her shoulder-length brown hair bobbed as she walked past.

Taking the bench before everyone in the room could stand up, the judge kindly waved for those who'd risen to be seated.

The Honorable Silvia Brown had presided over the Milford courthouse for more than a decade, after having run a small practice in an office located right off the oval. Prior to opening her own practice, she had served as a county prosecutor. She was no stranger to criminal matters, and Mason Walters preferred to have the case in front of someone like her.

Judge Brown surveyed the courtroom. "It appears we have quite a crowd today," she said, smiling to everyone.

"We haven't done a roll call yet," the bailiff informed her.

"Go right ahead," Judge Brown said.

The bailiff read off the parties to each case. Most of the matters were the state versus an individual who didn't have counsel. People stood to announce they were present, and the prosecutor nodded that he was assigned each case.

Steve Jenson was the prosecutor. He'd been a police officer who had gone to law school at night. Now, he served as the police prosecutor for the Town of Milford. Once a serious matter was ushered through the local court, it would move forward in superior court and a prosecutor from the County Attorney's

Office or the Attorney General's Office would take over.

When their matter was called, Mason stood and announced that he and his client were present. For the next matter Kyle Wentworth rose and did the same. The bailiff called Scott Bancroft's case, and Sam Makinson rose and told the judge the defense was present. Steve Jenson stood in for the state in all three cases.

Despite his background in law enforcement, Jenson's heavyset build and sarcastic grins were reminiscent of a college frat boy. He'd studied criminal justice at a local state college, and his behavior made Mason wonder if the guy had really majored in beer drinking.

There were a few matters called with public defenders assigned to them, and the lawyers went through the same routine.

A few matters had defendants called, who had not appeared before the court.

"What do you want to do about the no shows?" the bailiff asked the judge.

"Let's put them on for a second call," Judge Brown said. "If they don't appear for the afternoon session, we'll issue bench warrants."

"Will do," the bailiff said.

"We seem to have several private lawyers here today," Judge Brown said, looking at the prosecutor, then to Mason.

"They're here for a few related matters," Jenson said.

"What's on for today?" she asked.

"Arraignments," Jenson said. "We also need to set some calendar dates."

"That's all?" Judge Brown questioned, looking through some papers. "I have probable cause hearings noted as well."

"I figured we'd set calendar dates for them," Jenson said.

"You *figured*?" Judge Brown said.

"Yes, ma'am."

"Have you conferred with the other attorneys?"

"No. I just figured—"

"I'd like to hear from the defense lawyers."

Sam Makinson stood up. Then, Kyle Wentworth rose to his feet, and Mason followed suit. Kyle was in a pew on the right side of the courtroom, near the front. Mason was on the left side of the courtroom further back.

"Attorney Makinson, what do you have to say?" Judge Brown asked.

"We're fine with that approach, Your Honor."

Judge Brown next turned to Kyle Wentworth, likely because he was the next closest lawyer. "How about you?"

"That's fine with us."

Judge Brown nodded, then she looked further back into the courtroom. "Mr. Walters?"

"I'm afraid that we cannot agree with the prosecution's suggestion."

She frowned. Then, she turned to the bailiff. "I'll see counsel in chambers. The court will take a fifteen-minute recess. All of you in the gallery need to return promptly."

Judge Brown stood up and whisked off the bench, her robe flowing behind her.

The bailiff hustled to the door in the back of the courtroom, intending to hold the door for the judge. But the judge pushed through the doorway and disappeared down a corridor. Then the bailiff turned and stepped into the well of the courtroom.

"Counsel in the three related cases need to follow me," he said, hitching up his pants.

Mason leaned towards Tyler. "This will just take a minute."

"Is everything all right?" Tyler asked.

"Just a routine conference with the judge about next steps."

Sam Makinson led the way, followed by Kyle Wentworth and Steve Jenson. Mason pulled up the rear, as the lawyers walked single file out the back of the courtroom. The bailiff held the door open as they stepped into an interior hallway.

Once everyone was through, the lawyers paused to allow the bailiff a moment to take the lead. He trundled down the corridor with his weight shifting left and right. They walked past offices on the left with glass windows, where court personnel worked on files, copying, and mailing. Doorways on the right led to conference rooms, a printer station, and a few offices utilized by the presiding judges.

They reached an office in the back corner of the building. And then, the bailiff poked his head into the office. He nodded. Then he pressed the door wide open and motioned for the attorneys to enter.

The four lawyers funneled into the judge's chambers.

As the senior justice, Judge Brown was afforded a spacious office with windows overlooking the woods behind the courthouse. The other offices likely had views of the side parking lot. She sat behind a large desk, which faced them.

Judge Brown stood up and greeted them with a forced smile.

She wore a formal pantsuit. Her robe was hung on a coatrack near the door.

Mason was always surprised at how fast a judge could disrobe. Even for short conferences in chambers, they usually opted to take the robe off.

Various prints, degrees, and law licenses hung on the walls. A multicolored print of Abraham Lincoln hung on a wall between a bookcase and a window. Judge Brown liked to preside over matters as fairly as possible. Honest Abe was fitting.

"Please take a seat," Judge Brown said, motioning to three chairs situated in front of her desk.

Steve Jenson pushed ahead and took the first chair. Sam Makinson sat in the next chair, and Kyle Wentworth shoved his way into the third seat. The bailiff stepped away and returned with a chair on wheels, which he rolled up next to the others. Mason plopped down in the last seat.

"Anything else?" the bailiff asked the judge.

"No. That will be all."

He stepped outside, and eased the door closed behind him.

Judge Brown turned to Mason, and said, "So, what's the story?"

"It's pretty simple," Mason said. "My client isn't willing to waive any of his rights to a timely probable cause hearing, or a speedy trial."

She leaned forward and glanced at Jenson. "Are you prepared to go forward?"

He looked flabbergasted. "Your Honor..."

"Are you ready or not?"

"Well, I certainly didn't expect—"

"Yes or no."

"Yes, but I need to get witnesses here," Jenson said. "Like I was saying, we weren't anticipating going forward today."

Judge Brown sat back in her chair and considered his comments. "You understand that I could dismiss the case against Mr. Walters' client right now?"

"Ah, but...Your Honor."

She waved a hand at Jenson dismissively. "Don't worry, I'm not going to do that. But when you show up in my courtroom for a scheduled event, you better be ready to move forward," Judge Brown rasped, admonishing him like an addled schoolboy. "You should consult with counsel about continuances in *advance*."

"Understood, Your Honor." Jenson looked relieved.

Turning to Mason, "Without giving up attorney/client privilege or strategy, can you tell me why you're so insistent on going forward today?"

"Sure. They haven't got a shred of evidence on the felony murder charge."

Judge Brown smirked in amusement. "Well, I can't wait to see this."

"How do you want to proceed?" Mason asked.

"Can your witnesses be here at two o'clock?" she said to Jenson.

"Uh," he stuttered. "Yes."

"We'll handle the arraignments and bail for the other two cases," she said to Makinson. "So, you don't have to wait around."

"Thank you, Your Honor," Makinson said smoothly, like a dean of the bar.

"Mason, we'll see you back here after lunch," Judge Brown

said.

The lawyers waited to be dismissed before standing.

"That's all. You can go now," Judge Brown said, with the wave of a hand.

The lawyers rose in unison and bid the judge farewell. Mason opened the door and they all stepped into the hallway. The bailiff was waiting outside. He closed the door to the judge's office, then he led them back to the courtroom.

Walking down the corridor, Kyle Wentworth leaned over to Mason. He raised a hand to the side of his mouth and whispered, "*Mason?*" Kyle said, repeating Judge Brown. "Didn't know you were on a first name basis with the judge."

"You don't know a lot of things," Mason replied. "I've forgotten more of the law than you ever knew."

The slick lawyer laughed it off, but he looked worried.

CHAPTER TWENTY-SIX

MASON stepped from the corridor into the courtroom and broke from the bailiff and other lawyers. He walked across the well towards his eagerly awaiting client.

The other attorneys circled around the prosecution table, while Mason stepped through the gate. Listening to their banter, he picked up that they were scrambling to decide who to call as witnesses, and just how they were going to line them up on short notice.

Everyone was working in unison to pin the wrap on Mason's client.

Mason approached his client and Tyler stood up. The young man stepped into the aisle and said, "What's going on?"

"We can't talk here," Mason said.

"But—"

"Outside."

Mason plodded ahead to keep Tyler from talking further. *He's dumber than a bag of hammers,* Mason thought.

After they stepped from the courtroom into the hallway, Mason heard the door open and shut behind them. He turned and saw the man in the trucker's jacket eyeballing them. Mason grabbed Tyler by the arm and led him away from the other defendant so they wouldn't be overheard.

The man seemed to trace their footsteps.

Mason picked up his pace, heading for a vacant corner near

a window. He simply didn't want to get overheard by Wade Garrett or anyone else.

But Wade kept after them. He had an odd gleam in his eyes.

Mason turned to the man. "That's enough. We're trying to have a discussion. Please keep your distance."

The look in Wade's eyes changed into primal rage. He bull rushed Mason.

Mason stood his ground, as the man hurried towards him.

"You don't give me orders, Mr. Lawyer," Wade said, closing in on him.

"Listen, you can't let this matter get to you," Mason said, gesticulating, while trying to reason with the man. "You need to calm down."

Wade halted. He stood nose to nose with Mason, fuming and panting for breath.

"You need to step back," Mason said, holding his ground.

"Don't tell me what to do!" Wade yelled, while grabbing Mason by the arm.

Mason shook his arm free, then Wade clutched his tie. The thug pulled the tie tight around Mason's throat, choking him.

Wade was stocky and seemed to have the advantage over the wiry attorney.

Taking a step around Wade, the lawyer placed his right leg behind Wade's knee. Then, he pushed a shoulder into Wade's chest, and the blocky man tumbled to the floor, smacking his head on the tile. It seemed to daze him for a moment.

Mason readied himself for a fight, expecting Wade to jump up and come at him.

Carl had ventured up to the second-floor landing and hustled over. He stood near the fallen man. "What's going on here, Mason?" Carl said.

Wade shook it off and began scrambling to get back on his feet.

Placing a hand on Wade's shoulder, the burly security guard said, "You stay right there until I get this straightened out."

Wade sat on the floor with a smirk on his face.

"What's this all about?" Carl asked again.

"Just a minor altercation," Mason said. "Ain't that right?" he added, looking at Wade.

"Sure. That's right."

"You want to press any charges?" Carl said.

"No." Mason replied. "I think we're fine."

"You," Carl said to Wade, "go on and get out of here. Before I change my mind."

Wade scrambled to his feet and headed towards the restroom.

"Got my training at Parris Island," Carl said. "You?"

"Fort Benning, Georgia," Mason replied with a grin.

Carl chuckled and gave Mason a pat on the shoulder. "I'll leave you two alone," he said, then walked off towards the landing.

Mason turned to his client. Tyler looked frightened.

"We have a recess until this afternoon," Mason said. "Let's get out of here."

Tyler looked glum. "Where to?"

"We'll grab a coffee at the diner in the oval."

CHAPTER TWENTY-SEVEN

MASON entered a local diner with Tyler on his heel and found a seat in a booth away from the crowd. The regulars eyeballed them with interest.

A few minutes later, Dan approached and poured them some coffee.

"Lunch or breakfast?" Dan said.

Mason chuckled. It was late morning and he'd already eaten breakfast, and it was too early for lunch. "Why don't you give us a minute to figure this out."

"Sure thing, Mason," Dan said, turning away.

"People around here all seem to know you," Tyler said.

"I grew up in this town," Mason said. "I've spent most of my life here, except for a stint in the Army and going away to law school."

"Where did you go to law school?" Tyler asked, sipping coffee.

"UConn."

Tyler nodded, as if impressed.

Water pounded over the dam outside and a hum from the noise permeated into the diner. It was more noticeable during a lull in their conversation.

"Listen," Tyler finally said. "I'm a little nervous about how this is going down."

"You have good reason to be," Mason said.

"Really?"

"Sure. They have all the cannons pointed at you."

"Well, I'm also scared about having my trial first," Tyler said. "Wouldn't that just make them double down on me even more?"

"Might," Mason said.

Tyler's eyes grew wide. "Then why do it?"

"Because in a case like this," Mason said, "time isn't your friend."

"How so?"

"You don't need to give the police and prosecution more time to dig things up," Mason explained. "Heck, you don't need to give the others time to *plant* something else."

"So, you think I'm being set up."

Mason took a sip of coffee, then he sat back and considered the young man. He wanted to believe the kid was innocent, but he didn't feel like putting himself out there. "A criminal defense lawyer often has to go with what a client is telling him. If you didn't take part in the fire, then somebody left one of your gas cans at the scene."

"I've never brought a gas can to the mill," Tyler muttered.

Dan came back. "What will it be?"

"I'll go with eggs sunny side over," Mason said.

"You?" Dan said to Tyler.

"Guess, I'll just have the same."

Dan looked at Mason. "Toast and sausage?"

"Sure thing," Mason said, nodding.

Mason asked Tyler more about the outlook for the business and whether it had any hope of surviving had the fire not occurred. He also began to wonder if Jenkins had put the screws to anyone else.

Dan brought over their meals and left a slip for the bill. He didn't bother to ask who was paying.

While mopping up some yoke with his toast, Mason thought about how the diner was quaint and fit in with the oval. It was a quintessential center of a New England town, but few towns in the northeast actually had a town square like Milford.

Politicians often passed through the town, making a stop in the oval with photographs and film footage taken near the bandstand. The local news broadcast the weather with footage of the oval taken from a camera on the town hall.

The camera on the town hall, he thought.

"What is it?" Tyler asked, as if registering the lawyer was on to something.

"You live over by the tennis club, right?" Mason said.

"Sure. You've been there."

"And you told me that you went directly home when you left the mill."

"That's what happened."

"Well, there's a camera on the town hall. It might have footage of you driving through the oval on the night of the fire."

Tyler shook his head. "Afraid that won't help."

"Why not?" Mason asked, worried the kid wasn't playing it straight with him.

"Because I never drive through here on the way home at night," Tyler said. "I always take the bypass."

The Milford Bypass was a stretch of highway that circled around the town. It was used mostly for truckers, but people tended to use it to save time getting from one end of town to the other. Mason wondered if that were really the case, though.

There was a stretch of roadway that shot past the area where Tyler lived, so the kid would have to back track to get home. Plus, there was time spent getting on and off the bypass. Mason couldn't see how using the bypass would save Tyler any significant time.

Mason wondered if a jury would just think the kid made it up, or worse, took the bypass to avoid timing of his movements.

CHAPTER TWENTY-EIGHT

MASON and Tyler walked into an empty courtroom. The lights were turned down and it appeared to be finished with business for the day.

"Are we early?" Tyler asked.

"No." Mason knew the difference between an empty courtroom due to people straggling back from lunch and one shut down for the day.

"What's going on?" Tyler said, nervously.

"That's what I'd like to know," Mason said. But even as he spoke the words, he had a suspicion of what had gone down. "I'll go check for a bailiff."

Just as Mason turned away from his client, intending to head back out into the hallway, the door in the back of the courtroom opened. A bailiff stepped through holding a slip of paper in his hand.

"Oh, there you are," the bailiff said.

"What gives?" Mason said, approaching the bailiff.

"Judge Brown instructed me to give you this," the bailiff said, handing over the document.

"Thanks," Mason said, taking the piece of paper.

Perusing the document, it was a court pleading stating that the charges against Tyler had been *Nolle Prossed*, dismissed without prejudice.

"What is it?" Tyler demanded.

"The prosecutor dismissed the charges without prejudice."

"Why?"

"He probably figured there wasn't enough evidence," Mason said. "They'll wait for the autopsy report then decide what to do."

"Does that mean the case was dropped?" Tyler asked, hopefully.

"It means that you'll be indicted by a grand jury."

***

LEAVING the courtroom, Mason took a seat on a bench in the hallway, while the bailiff locked the courtroom doors. Tyler stood lingering before him.

The courthouse was a stark contrast from the hectic morning cattle call sessions. Most of the matters had been handled by the two presiding judges. Now, the place was almost empty. A few stragglers loitered in the hallways, wrapping up their affairs.

"I don't get what's going on," Tyler said.

"Why don't you take a seat?" Mason said, motioning to the bench.

Tyler reluctantly sat down beside him.

"Dismissal of the felony murder charge was a foregone conclusion," Mason said. "They didn't have a medical report indicating Jenkins had even been murdered."

"So, this is a good result?" asked Tyler.

"I'm not certain."

"Why?"

"The state is transitioning away from probable cause hearings in the District Courts," Mason explained. "We are moving towards all felony charges being handled through grand juries. That means that you and your counsel do not get to confront the charges. A prosecutor just stands before a grand jury and tells his or her side of the case. Indictment is almost certain when you don't have an opportunity to advocate.

Furthermore, they can undergo a grand jury inquiry without even advising you that it's happening."

"Really?"

"You'll just get new charges in the mail, or the police will show up to arrest you."

Apprehension consumed the young client's countenance. It was like the kid fully understood that new charges would be filed, and they would include murder.

CHAPTER TWENTY-NINE

A MONTH passed from the time Tyler's case was dismissed. Mason had put the file aside because nothing had transpired. There hadn't been a single development, and there wasn't any news about the companion matters, either.

Sitting in his office on a Friday afternoon, as snowflakes whisked past the windows overlooking Main Street, Mason worked on a routine motion and planned to wrap up for the day. He had pleadings spread across the top of his oak desk as he clacked away on his laptop. Tyler Cummings was the furthest thing from his mind.

The phone rang and Diane answered. She muttered, "Okay." Then, she appeared in Mason's doorway with a concerned look on her face. "Do you have a moment?" she said.

"Apparently so," Mason replied with a chuckle.

"Tyler Cummings is on the line. He's been indicted."

"You can put him through," Mason said, pushing his laptop aside.

The extension for his office line rang.

Mason slid the phone closer and answered. "Hello, this is Mason Walters."

"Mr. Walters, this is Tyler Cummings."

"You've got some news?"

"Afraid I've been indicted," Tyler said, sounding despondent.

"That's what I expected. Can you look at the paperwork and

read me the charges?"

"Well, that's the funny thing..."

"Go ahead."

"They charged me with arson and murder," Tyler said. "It's not conspiracy to commit arson and felony murder like the last time."

"What is stated for the murder charge?" Mason asked.

"It says RSA 603:1."

"You sure it doesn't say RSA 603:1-a?"

"No. There isn't anything after the one," Tyler said.

Mason sat back and his oak desk chair creaked. He didn't respond right away.

The charges really had been changed. Tyler was facing arson and premeditated murder. It wasn't a felony murder situation, which can be beaten by showing the defendant did not commit the underlying crime. The prosecution must have obtained evidence that Jenkins was deliberately killed and didn't just suffer harm from the fire.

"Are you there?" Tyler said.

"Yup. Just thinking."

Mason glanced out the window. Snow had begun to collect on the streetlamps, and it covered the sidewalks. He was thinking about heading out for the day before driving conditions plummeted. Now, he had to decide how much handholding the kid needed.

"I don't like this," Tyler said. "Not one bit."

"Nothing you can do about it."

"What's the game plan?"

These things always happen on a Friday afternoon, Mason thought.

A car slid to a stop at a traffic light outside.

"Listen, I would have you come by here to talk about things," Mason said. "But it's getting a little slippery out. We should plan to touch base next week. I'll send you an email to set up a time for a meeting."

Tyler paused before answering. "Okay," he said. But he

sounded miffed.

***

MASON hung up the phone and it immediately rang. He looked at the caller ID, expecting that Tyler was calling him again. It was the Attorney General's Office.

He reached for the phone, and said, "Mason Walters."

"Hey, Attorney Walters. This is Cody Harper with the Attorney General's Office."

Harper had dirty blonde hair and a square jaw. He was a slick lawyer on the rise and relished every chance he could get his mug in the newspapers and on television.

"Nice of you to call," Mason said.

"Do you have a minute?"

"Just a few," Mason said. "How can I help you?"

"We served your client, Tyler Cummings," Harper said.

"And?"

"Our office is planning to conduct a formal scene investigation of the site. You're welcome to attend. You can bring an expert if you'd like."

"When do you plan to do this?"

"That's why I'm calling. It would be this Tuesday."

"What sort of tests are you planning?"

"The typical cause and origin investigation. Maybe some further crime scene review."

Mason thought about it. They had investigated all of this prior to the indictment. He figured this was solely to gather select materials in order to get experts to agree on testing protocols. The reason they'd invite him would be to avoid a dispute at trial about their testing.

"What time?" Mason said.

"I was thinking 9:00 AM."

"Okay, I'll see you there," Mason replied. Then, he hung up the phone before Harper could say anything further. Mason planned to obtain what he could from the site visit, but he wasn't planning to agree to testing protocols.

He was born at night, but it wasn't last night.

***

MASON picked up the phone and called Ray Jefferson. The private investigator answered straight away.

"What do we know about Scott Bancroft's father?" Mason asked.

"Not much, other than he's a successful businessman in the Souhegan Valley."

"Let's open a file on him and see what we can dig up."

"Sure thing," Ray said. "What are you looking for?"

"Any signs of debt," Mason said.

CHAPTER THIRTY

NEXT WEEK, Mason saw his wife off to work, then he puttered around the house making eggs for breakfast. The site visit was in the opposite direction from the office, so he planned to head straight there from his house.

Mason had spoken with Tyler's parents on the telephone and they managed to scrape together the hefty amount of funds for his bail relative to the new charges. They had used their savings to pay the balance of the retainer and had to borrow from other family members to come up with the money.

After a clean shave and a shower, he dressed in lined jeans and a flannel shirt. He put on wool socks and a pair of Sorel boots. Mason gave Benny a pat on the head, slipped into a parka, then he stepped outside into a frigid morning. Clouds from his breath formed in the cold air, as he walked to the carriage shed carrying his knapsack by the handle. Opening the door to his sport wagon, he slid inside and shut the door. It wasn't much warmer in the car. He put the backpack into the front passenger seat.

He fired up the engine and flicked on the buttons for the heated seat and heated steering wheel. Mason adjusted the controls for the temperature, then he backed the car out of the shed.

By the time he reached the end of his long driveway, the steering wheel and seat were warmed up. He turned onto the roadway and headed towards Milford. Speeding along the rural highway, the trees and exposed grass were covered in frost. Everything that wasn't frozen over was covered in snow. It was like a winter wonderland.

They picked a fine day for a site visit, Mason thought.

Mason listened to the local public radio station and drove along with light traffic.

Eventually, he reached the Milford town line and decided to take the bypass. He checked the clock on his dashboard and made a mental note of the time. The onramp to the bypass was similar to the type used for a highway. Cut through ledge, the roadway was flanked by immense rockfaces. Mason had seen rock climbers practicing on rocks in the past. People risked life and limb to climb up a rockface when a perfectly suitable trail could get them to the same place. Mason opted for safer activities, like hiking and fishing.

Nothing wrong with standing in a stream, the trout bum thought.

The onramp merged onto a highway with exits. It wasn't divided and only had one lane in each direction. Approaching the first exit, Mason concluded that it led into the center of town and couldn't serve as a shortcut to Tyler's house. He'd been correct in thinking the closest exit to Tyler's house was a location that would cause the young man to double back.

He also noticed the bypass took him out and around the town, like traveling along a semi-circle, compared to roads that were a straight shot through town.

Mason got bogged down behind a slow-moving car and hoped it would exit. There was too much traffic coming in the opposite direction to pass. This was part of the reason he typically opted to drive through town. That and the fact the bypass had nothing to look at but pine trees.

When he finally reached the end of the bypass, it turned to two lanes. He passed the slow-moving vehicle.

Mason banged a left after stopping for a light. He drove along the rural highway with businesses intermittently lining the left side of the road. A river rushed along the righthand side of the roadway. Icy waters washed over smooth stones in the riverbed.

Crossing over the Wilton town line, Mason checked the clock

on his dashboard. He'd forgotten to look at the time when he exited the bypass.

I'll just run the time from the mill, he decided.

He rounded a curve in the roadway and the grade suddenly became steep.

Ahead of him, an old brick factory stood on the edge of a rushing river. Most of the roof had burned away and the tops of the brick walls were blackened by soot. The place resembled a bombed-out building that had been shelled during World War II.

He spotted the gravel entrance and banged a right.

Mason crossed the river by driving over an old stone bridge, then he pulled into a large dirt parking lot, covered in a blanket of snow. The area closest to the building was crammed with vehicles: a State Police crime scene van, a few cruisers, a couple unmarked police cars, a pickup truck, a Cadillac Escalade, and an aging Saab convertible.

Makinson and Wentworth, Mason thought looking at the Cadillac and Saab.

He figured the pickup truck belonged to an outside expert retained by the state.

Mason parked and headed towards the main entrance to the old factory. It had a bell tower situated near the front door. The tower shot above the roofline and had a large clockface lodged into it. Gusts of wind whipped through the valley and howled over the river.

A group of people were huddled near the main entrance.

Cody Harper held court in front of the doorway. He wore a suit and tie, a black trench coat, and his dress shoes were caked in snow and ice. Wentworth looked like a model from a J.Crew catalogue, while Makinson wore a suit and wool overcoat. The old lawyer had donned a pair of L.L. Bean boots, prepared for the environment. All the police officers were in uniform and wore winter boots. A civilian wore clothing for the outdoors and a ski jacket.

The only person who wasn't dressed for the occasion was the lawyer leading the party.

Mason was just relieved that Harper hadn't leaked news about the site visit to the press. He trucked over and joined the group.

Cody Harper smiled kindly at Mason, like a natural born politician.

"Morning," Harper said to Mason.

Mason nodded, but he didn't smile. "Good morning."

Everyone else in the group nodded a greeting. Kyle Wentworth stepped over and shook Mason's hand. The police officers were situated on the outskirts of the circle. They looked like they had been up for quite some time. Mason figured the tired faces meant they had already been perusing the place before the site visit got underway.

If they'd found anything good, they'd look a lot more chipper, Mason concluded.

"Do you have an expert coming?" Harper asked Mason.

Mason shook his head. "Not at this time."

"You'll need to be the one to agree on the testing protocols," Harper said.

"I've thought about that," Mason replied. "For today, we just need to agree upon a process for taking the samples and gathering three sets. A set for testing, a set for the prosecution, and a set for the defense. We can decide the testing protocols after your expert provides us with a written outline of what he plans to do."

Mason was thinking that the expert would likely apply standard ASTM approaches, which were established engineering and scientific test procedures.

Harper frowned. "Okay. Let's see how it goes."

The comment was noncommittal, and the young prosecutor appeared dismayed. But there really wasn't much he could do. Mason had figured a way around the prosecutor's goal for this site visit.

"We're going to head inside," Harper said.

A police officer entered the building and the prosecutor's expert trailed behind him.

"You need to follow the procession," Harper added. "And turn on the flashlights to your cellphones."

Mason fished his phone out of a pocket and clicked on the light.

Stepping inside the building, he took up the rear of a line of people slowly walking into the mill. It wasn't as dark as he had expected. Light shone through the opening in the roof and through burnt sections on the old factory flooring. A large area had burned through the planks of each floor of the mill. There was a hole about twenty feet in diameter running all the way through the roof.

The place smelled like charred wood and melted plastic, more of a toxic scent than the aroma of a fireplace. Mason wished he'd brought a bandana or something to cover his face.

A police officer led them to a narrow staircase near an outside wall. It was covered in soot and burnt in places, but it looked solid. They headed down the stairs, which reached a landing, turned and headed to the concrete floor of the basement.

Descending into the space blocked out the wind and brought Mason some relief from the bitter cold. But the stench grew more pronounced. Charred machinery filled the space, along with debris from burnt support beams and plank flooring. The detritus of materials from the floors above lay in heaps on the basement floor.

Toxic fumes wafted through the space, with the occasional breeze that blew through broken windows, located about six feet above the basement walls.

Harper accompanied a crime scene officer and his expert deeper into the space. They clearly meant to undertake further investigation alone. Mason watched as the expert took measurements and photographs. There were classic "V" patterns on several areas of the walls.

Accidental fires typical start at one location with a single "V" pattern. Then signs of the fire spreading through contact with combustible materials follows. Several "V" patterns reflected multiple origins of fire, which was a classic sign of arson. Test results would likely reveal the use of accelerants at the source of each fire origin.

Mason reached a couple of conclusions. First, the fire wasn't started by a professional. Professional arsonists start fires by making it look accidental. They play around with wiring, so the electricity causes an arch. They also remove fuses and flip breakers. Sometimes they pile flammable materials in an area, making it look like stored materials, so when the fire starts, it gets enhanced once it reaches the stockpile of flammables.

Second, whoever started the fire had ample access to the building. All this caused Mason to question the entire situation. Surely, the business owners wouldn't have been so rash as to a kneejerk reaction. They'd recently concluded a meeting with Jenkins and then the place was burned in haste.

Maybe someone else had it in for Jenkins? Mason wondered.

***

AFTER watching the expert take samples from each origin of fire, Mason saw the expert walk over to the breaker box. The expert shook his head, then took a few photographs.

Then the expert followed the electrical lines from the breaker box and discovered a few old-fashioned fuse boxes. He took more photographs, then he nodded to Cody Harper, like he was through.

Harper showed Mason the various samples taken from the scene. "We'll send you an email with the proposed protocols," Harper said.

"Sounds good," Mason replied.

This all could have been done through a crime scene investigation and use of the local fire marshal. Mason knew they wanted to bait him into accepting testing protocols, but if the expert utilized standard tests, the step wouldn't have been much help.

Something else is in play, Mason concluded.

The procession headed topside. Mason stepped into the frigid morning air and took a deep breath, all too happy to leave the noxious fumes behind. Harper reiterated that Mason and the other lawyers would be receiving an email about the protocols. Then the prosecutor thanked everyone for their time.

Just as the group was starting to disburse and head back to their vehicles, a loud crack resounded through the valley.

A burning sensation tore through Mason's upper left arm.

Mason hit the deck and blood leaked into the snow from his shoulder.

The officers ducked behind the crime scene van, while the three attorneys stood dumbfounded.

"Get behind cover," Mason called to the lawyers.

Mason crawled on his belly over to a nearby car. Then, he sat behind a tire and wriggled out of his parka. He unbuttoned his shirt and slid his left arm out. A bullet had grazed his deltoid, and blood gushed from the wound.

***

WADE GARRETT sat on the edge of a hillside crouched beside a tree holding a hunting rifle. He was situated about five hundred yards from the entrance to the mill.

The shot had echoed through the entire valley.

He figured that it had been fired from the opposite hillside.

Someone else wants that lawyer dead, Wade thought.

Although his rifle hadn't been fired, he didn't want to be implicated in this crime. Not if he hadn't pulled the trigger.

Wade eased back up the hill and climbed over the crest out of sight.

He bolted through the trees to the country road below. Then, he opened the door to his truck and slid the rifle behind the seat. Wade climbed into the cab and fired up the engine. Shifting into gear, he did a hasty three-point turn and barreled the truck back to Milford.

Wade planned to put as much distance between him and the

mill as possible.

Crossing the town line, he didn't see any cruisers in his rearview mirror. Wade slowed down and decided to head over to the diner for some coffee. It would make for the best alibi.

He didn't want to be seen driving into the oval from Route 101A, which led from Wilton where the mill was located. Wade turned left onto North River Road and headed uphill towards the sleepy town of Mount Vernon. Then he cut over to Route 13, planning to take it south down to the diner.

Just as he returned to flat land, he glanced over at the convenience store nestled in a snow-covered meadow near Perkins Street.

"Well I'll be damned," Wade muttered to himself.

Scott Bancroft was parked at the pumps putting gas in his truck, trying to look casual. But he seemed anything but relaxed. In fact, he looked quite suspicious.

CHAPTER THIRTY-ONE

MASON was treated by an EMT at the scene but refused transport to the hospital. He found himself seated in an interrogation room at the nearby Milford police station.

Cody Harper was seated across from him, accompanied by Detective Sergeant LeClair and Officer Durham. They were seated in a small cinderblock room with a metal table and metal chairs. This room didn't stink and was probably reserved for meeting with people reporting crimes and giving witness statements.

"Tell us who you think shot you," Harper said.

Mason shrugged. "Afraid I really can't say anything to you."

"Why not?" Harper really sounded interested to know.

"You're opposing counsel in an ongoing matter," Mason said. "Anything that I say could reveal my impressions about the matter, or possibly reveal strategic considerations."

"How so?" Harper kept at it.

Mason considered the situation. A prosecutor really didn't have to contend with the ethical dilemmas of an attorney in private practice. Harper probably couldn't fathom how such a discussion could possibly open a can of worms.

Mason shrugged. "If you don't understand, I really can't help you."

"You're committing obstruction of justice," LeClair chimed in.

"Afraid not. I don't have any material information to report."

"Then talking to us won't reveal any attorney/client information," Harper said.

"You really don't get it," Mason said, smiling condescendingly.

"What?"

"That my impressions and speculations about this could relate to an ongoing matter. It makes them per se protected."

"So, you're not going to talk to us?" Harper said, testily.

"No. I'm not."

"Then you're wasting our time here."

"Probably."

Mason used the opportunity to put an end to the meeting. He rose from his chair and slowly walked towards the door.

Officer Durham eyeballed him.

For a moment, Mason wondered if the cop was going to grab him and shove him back into the chair. He reached the door and turned the knob.

"Afraid someone has to escort you out," LeClair said.

"Let's go then."

Mason opened the door and stepped into the hallway, waiting for someone to walk him out. A moment later, Officer Durham stepped from the room.

"This way," he said, heading down the corridor.

Mason followed him to a door that led into the lobby. Officer Durham opened the door and held it until Mason walked past.

Once the door closed behind him, Mason hurried for the front door.

He noticed the young cop at the reception window staring as he left the building.

Outside, he reached into his coat pocket and pulled out his cellphone, as he walked towards his car. Mason found Ray Jefferson in his contacts. Hitting the button, Mason called the private investigator.

The phone rang a few times, then Jefferson answered. "Mason, that you?"

"Sure is."

"Funny that you called. I was just about to call you."

"Give me a moment," Mason said, climbing into his car.

Jefferson waited, probably realizing that Mason wanted to be in a secure spot.

"Okay," Mason said. "Tell me what you've got."

"You won't believe this," Jefferson said. Then, he filled Mason in on the details, which caused Mason to sit back and listen.

"Good work," Mason said. "Now, let's look into the girlfriends?"

CHAPTER THIRTY-TWO

AWEEK later, the prosecution sent over a Bankers Box jampacked with discovery for Tyler's upcoming trial.

Mason sat in a conference room with the box of discovery on top of his oak library table. Tyler sat across from him in an antique courthouse chair. Prior to the meeting, Mason had gone through everything with a fine-tooth comb. They had gotten the autopsy report on Jenkins' death, as well as the crime scene investigation, the fire cause and origin report, scene photographs, and witness statements.

"Any surprises?" Tyler asked. He didn't seem like he wanted to roll up his sleeves and dig through the box.

"Someone shot Jenkins in the head," Mason said. "A small caliber pistol, so the injury didn't show up until the autopsy report. These are country police officers. They don't see homicide cases very often."

Tyler sat there looking dumbfounded. "Homicide?" he said.

"Makes the stakes go up a bit. They tied it to a kidnapping hostage charge, so they must think that Jenkins was taken and brought to the factory basement while he was still alive."

"Hostage?" Tyler muttered.

"We need to focus on going over what we know and don't know," Mason said. "This is bad news, but we have to move past it."

Tyler straightened up. "So, what else is in there?"

"What's surprising is what isn't in there," Mason said.

"How so?" asked Tyler.

"There's no murder weapon. Nothing alleged to have been used to ignite the fires. And the witness statements are scant."

"So, the case is purely circumstantial?"

Mason didn't like the sound of that. Tyler had gone from meek and mild to a jailhouse lawyer overnight. "Many cases are presented by the prosecution," Mason said, "and *won*, based upon circumstantial evidence. All that really means is they don't have an eyewitness to the crime."

"Doesn't the lack of an eyewitness make the case weak?"

"Let's not get into that sort of thinking," Mason said.

"What sort of thinking?" Tyler asked, petulantly.

"The sort of thinking that views the prosecution's case as weak," Mason said. "You're on trial for arson and murder. You start being dismissive of their case and get too cocky, and the whole thing can go down the drain, and you with it."

Tyler nodded. "I didn't mean to be dis… dismissive."

Now, the kid looked dejected, like someone had just killed his dog.

"Let's talk about process," Mason said, changing the subject.

"Sure." Tyler sat up, paying close attention.

Now, he's like a college kid attending a mid-term review, Mason thought.

Mason spent the rest of the meeting explaining how a jury trial is undertaken. He described the process for jury selection, opening statements, the prosecution's case, and how the defense case would be set up with bookends, where Mason would have a strong witness testify first and a strong witness testify last. The witnesses that are harder to control would testify in-between the strong witnesses.

He didn't get into discussion about how a directed verdict is handled, or the steps taken to preserve rights for an appeal. All of that would get too technical, and Mason just wanted the kid to focus on two things: looking innocent at counsel table, and presenting well if they decided to call Tyler as a witness.

CHAPTER THIRTY-THREE

A MONTH later, Mason found himself standing at counsel table in Hillsborough County Superior Court – South, located in Nashua a few blocks from his office.

Tyler stood next to him looking nervous and guilty as sin.

Cody Harper was positioned behind the prosecutor's table appearing cocksure of a win. A younger attorney, Susan Atkins, was standing next to him, and she appeared slightly nervous. Mason wondered if it was inexperience or something more that caused her diffidence.

The courthouse had been remodeled within the past decade and it had similar features to the Milford District Court. The bench, witness stand, and jury box were comprised of maple with a light finish. The counsel tables and chairs were made of oak, as were the pews in the gallery. The walls were painted sage green with an occasional accent around the bench and jury box painted in a dark, hunter green. The carpet was woven with hints of green.

New Hampshire state buildings opted for green most of the time, likely as a tribute to its heritage in the lumber industry.

The gallery had scatterings of spectators. Some were the press, others were family members of the accused, while still others were lawyers with an interest in this case. Judge Thomas Wakefield, III would preside over the case. He was a fourth-generation lawyer in the state and a second-generation judge. His father's portrait hung in the superior courthouse in Concord, New Hampshire.

Everyone was quiet as they waited for the judge to enter into the courtroom.

A door in the back finally opened, and the judge stepped inside.

"All rise," a bailiff called out.

The lawyers and the people in the gallery came to attention. Tyler took a moment to gather what was happening and finally scrambled to his feet.

Judge Wakefield walked slowly towards the bench. He had a full head of graying hair, cut close and parted to the right. The judge exuded confidence, and his lean build reflected a personality that had everything under control. He was in his late fifties and knew the law and understood evidence, as if he'd memorized a treatise on the subject.

Like many members of long-standing New Hampshire families, he'd gone to the University of New Hampshire. After graduating college, he made the typical move and went to law school in Boston, settling upon Boston University. He worked as an Assistant County Prosecutor for a few years before taking a position at a prominent New Hampshire firm. The firm's main office was located in a large granite building in Manchester and resembled the Lincoln Memorial, with large pillars on the front.

Judge Wakefield took the bench and glanced around at the gallery. Then, he looked at the lawyers, and said, "I understand the panel is ready to come through. Are there any pressing matters?"

Cody Harper straightened up. "Your Honor, we moved to quash trial subpoenas issued by the defense."

Judge Wakefield turned to the defense table. "Counsel?"

"We have merely subpoenaed third-parties with documents for impeachment purposes," Mason said.

"The motion is reserved," Judge Wakefield said, matter-of-factly. "I'll decide on them as the evidence comes in during trial."

"But—" Harper stammered.

"Another word and I'll deny the motion altogether."

Harper lowered his head and knew when to bite his tongue.

The judge's ruling meant that various entities would be turning over their documents to Mason at the first scheduled break. Representatives of the businesses he had subpoenaed were in the courtroom waiting for the ruling. They would be all too happy to dump the documents on Mason and clear out without taking the stand. This meant he could use the documents during the prosecution's case.

Mason had to hold back a satisfied grin.

Judge Wakefield looked at a bailiff in the back of the courtroom. "Let's bring in the panel," the judge said.

The bailiff propped the courtroom doors open. Then another bailiff led a procession of prospective jurors into the courtroom. Both bailiffs asked the people seated in the gallery to give up their seats until jury selection was concluded. This caused a swarm of people to funnel out of the courtroom, as members of the panel filled all the seats in the gallery.

Mason turned and faced the prospective jurors. He nudged Tyler to do the same. The prosecutors followed suit.

Despite having obtained a copy of Jury Questionnaires from the clerk's office, Mason couldn't discern anyone seated before him from the information on the forms. Each prospective juror was required to state their name, address, educational background, occupation, and connections with law enforcement and the legal community, as well as any prior criminal or civil legal matters.

The gallery simply resembled a group of people one might see running errands on the weekend. Most were dressed informally, with the exception of a few men in sports coats and ties and a few women wearing skirts.

Judge Wakefield introduced himself and most of the jurors smiled pleasantly.

They always like the judge, Mason thought.

After a brief introduction, the judge read the names of the attorneys, the defendant, and all the witnesses and asked the panel whether they knew anyone.

One woman reluctantly raised her hand.

"You may approach," Judge Wakefield said. Then, he motioned for counsel to join them.

Mason and Harper reached the bench and stood a few feet apart.

The prospective juror walked up and smiled kindly at Mason. She stood looking up at the judge expectantly. Walking up to the bench and standing in front of a room full of onlookers appeared to make her nervous.

"Do you know anyone involved with this case?" the judge said.

"Well, not personally," she replied. "But I've seen Mr. Harper on television."

Figures, Mason thought and frowned.

"Can you be impartial?" asked the judge.

"I suppose so. See, I'm new to all of this and felt that maybe I should mention it."

"Why don't you step back, so we can discuss this," the judge said.

When the potential juror stepped back, Mason and Harper closed up the space and stood close to the microphone housed in the top of the bench.

"I'm inclined to keep her," Judge Wakefield said. "What do you two think?"

"The State is satisfied with her objectivity," Harper said.

The judge looked at Mason. "You?"

"We have a full panel here, Your Honor," Mason said. "Her response to your question was she *supposes* that she can be objective. That's not a definitive statement. We've got a murder trial here. This isn't the time to seat a juror who might have been influenced by seeing the prosecutor on the evening news."

Judge Wakefield nodded. "Okay. Step aside."

The two lawyers made a path for the prospective juror to come forward.

"You may approach," the judge said.

She walked up looking less nervous.

"This is what we're going to do," the judge said. "We're not going to seat you for this trial. If your name gets called, raise your hand, then we'll select another person from the panel. This courthouse is drawing a jury for another matter in the next courtroom, so you might still get picked for that case."

"Okay," she said, forcing a smile.

"You haven't done anything wrong here," the judge assured her.

"Thanks." She smiled again.

"You may sit down."

The prospective juror headed to the gallery and the lawyers returned to their tables.

Judge Wakefield read a short description of the case. Then, he proceeded to ask voir dire questions, which had been prepared and reviewed with the attorneys in advance of trial. The gist of it was to determine if anyone on the panel held a bias and to find out if serving on the jury would cause a hardship.

Several prospective jurors raised their hands in response to the question about hardship.

The judge inquired with each of them one at a time. A couple of them were teachers who felt serving on the jury might cause an impact on their students. There was a doctor who felt rescheduling patients would cause a problem, and a woman told the judge that she didn't get sick time or vacation time from work because she had just started a new job. Judge Wakefield excused them all. He didn't ask the lawyers about the teachers or the woman without vacation time. They did confer about the doctor.

To Mason's surprise, Harper didn't want him on the jury. Having a doctor on the jury pool could help the defense with medical issues. But the idea of seating a high-level professional who didn't want to be on the jury wasn't palatable to Mason.

Judge Wakefield ultimately decided not to sit the doctor.

Once the initial review of the jury panel was concluded, the judge took a short break and allowed everyone to stretch out.

The next step was to actually seat the jury. Suddenly, the case had moved into a performance stage, where the lawyers had to put on a show. Mason felt his pulse race with anxiety.

CHAPTER THIRTY-FOUR

MASON stood next to Harper alongside the judge's bench as the trial moved forward in the jury selection process.

"Our approach is to sit eighteen jurors," Judge Wakefield said. "We select them at random. Then you both have an opportunity for individual voir dire. Preemptory challenges are alternated between the two of you. Any questions?"

"No," Mason said.

"What happens if we excuse six jurors?" Harper asked.

Judge Wakefield scowled at Harper. "Then we seat a couple more from the panel."

Mason restrained himself from chiming in.

The sessions clerk set a clear plastic bin on the edge of the judge's bench. It was loaded with slips that had the name of each juror printed on the front.

She reached her hand into the bin and extracted a slip. Then she slid it into a slot on a narrow board next to the number one. Afterward, she called out the juror's name and the person took a seat in the jury box.

This process was repeated until twelve people were seated in the box.

A bailiff rolled six chairs in front of the jury box, and the process was continued until eighteen people were seated.

"Mr. Harper, you may question the jurors," Judge Wakefield said.

Cody Harper stood up and walked over to the well of the courtroom. He flashed a politician's smile, and several jurors returned the favor. Harper wore a blue suit, white shirt, and red and blue rep tie. His shoes were polished. His clothing was pressed with new creases. The man looked like he was fit for prime time.

"My name is Cody Harper," he said. "And I'm an Assistant Attorney General for the State of New Hampshire."

A few jurors smiled in response to his introduction. His position garnered respect.

"Do any of you distrust the police?" Harper asked.

He's started with a whopper, Mason thought.

The question caused a few of the jurors to pucker their faces, as if such a blanket view would be offensive to the ordinary person.

Harper smiled at them, as if indicating *good job.*

"Do any of you harbor any grudges against prosecutors?"

Several jurors shook their heads and grinned as if the question was preposterous.

"Do any of you have difficulty with making a person convicted of a crime pay the penalty established by the law?"

A few jurors considered the question with confused looks on their faces.

"Juror number five," Harper said. "Do you have a problem with the notion that a person convicted of a crime will be sentenced by the judge?"

"No, sir," juror five said. "I do not."

"What about you, juror number nine?" Harper said.

"I do not."

And so it went for an hour and a half of Harper grilling the potential jurors. He asked questions that were somewhat repetitive. He also singled out jurors even when no one raised a hand.

When Harper finally concluded his voir dire and sat down, Judge Wakefield looked at Mason. "Do you think you'll be long? I'm just wondering about breaking for lunch."

Mason shook his head. "I'll be quick."

Judge Wakefield smiled. "All right, then."

Mason stood up and walked in front of the jury. He appeared like a country gentleman, with a gray suit, blue and maroon rep tie, and a First Infantry Division lapel pin. Mason's thinning hair was combed over, and his black shoes were polished, but they had a few scuff marks.

He presented like someone who had spent a lot of time in front of juries, but also like someone who puttered around a workshop doing his own carpentry work. There wasn't anything flashy about him. Mason was someone that you could trust.

"I'll be quick," Mason told the jurors.

"As the judge previously introduced me. I'm Mason Walters. I represent the defendant, Tyler Cummings in this matter." Mason pointed to Tyler. "I've just got a couple of questions."

Most of the jurors smiled, relieved they weren't going to get grilled.

"Can you remain objective until you hear *all* of the evidence?"

Every single juror smiled and nodded at him.

"Does anyone have a problem with following the standard of beyond a reasonable doubt?" Mason asked, scanning each juror.

They weren't as enthusiastic as the last question, but no one raised a hand.

He didn't want to single them out and make anyone feel uncomfortable. It was better to leave them with a little distaste for Harper.

Mason looked them over again. "That's all I have."

All the jurors smiled at being let off the hook.

Rather than head back to his table, Mason glanced at the judge to await further instruction.

Judge Wakefield motioned for the lawyers to attend a sidebar conference.

Approaching the bench, Mason watched as Harper fumbled navigating past a podium, which was located between the counsel tables.

Mason took up a position, so the jury had a clear view of Harper when he got to the bench.

"Do you have any challenges?" the judge asked Harper.

Harper glanced at his notepad. "Juror number five," Harper said.

"Do you have any challenges?" the judge asked Mason.

Mason had reviewed the Jury Questionnaires closely prior to the trial date. He had also considered the ideal juror and the least favorable juror.

The least favorable would be an engineer. Engineers tend to follow the rules and look at things methodically. An engineer would frown upon the bad business practices carried out at the mill. The most favorable juror would be someone inclined to question authority. A small business owner, or a person with a prior issue with the police would question the police and prosecution.

"Juror number eleven," Mason whispered. He was a mechanical engineer.

The judge turned to the jurors and told jurors number five and eleven that they could return to the panel. Two people got up and scooted past the others, then filed out of the jury box. Both of them looked disappointed, like maybe they had inferred from the dismissal they had done something wrong.

"Anyone else?" the judge asked the lawyers.

"Number nine," Harper said. And it came out loud enough for people to hear.

"I'm good," Mason said.

"Juror number nine," the judge said. "You may be excused."

She was heavyset and shuffled out of the jury box, then she trundled back to the gallery.

"Anyone else?" the judge said to Harper.

"None."

"You?"

"None," Mason said.

"All right." The judge spun and faced the jurors. "Juror number thirteen. You can be seated in seat number five. Juror number fourteen, please move to seat number nine. And juror number fifteen, you can take a seat in number eleven."

Jurors instructed to relocate got up and moved into their respective seats.

Three people sat in the remaining chairs in front of the jury box. They looked confused, as if wondering what would become of them. Mason and Harper returned to their tables.

"We have three people that are not in the jury box," Judge Wakefield said. "You will serve as alternates on this jury."

They all nodded, accepting the role.

"We'll have the bailiff set you up with seats next to the jury box, so you can view the trial."

A bailiff headed over, planning to get the seating situated.

Judge Wakefield turned and faced the lawyers. "We're going to take our lunch break at this time." He looked at the clock. "Please return at 1:30 for opening statements."

CHAPTER THIRTY-FIVE

MASON packed up his bag and looked at Tyler. The kid was in a state of shock and didn't seem to register they were clearing out for lunch.

"Come on," Mason said, putting on his coat. "We need to regroup and grab lunch."

Tyler nodded. "Oh… Okay," he said.

A few people walked over to the railing. Each of them held a stack of documents.

"Those for me?" Mason said to them.

"Yup," a stout woman said.

"Sure thing," another woman replied.

"Yes, sir," a wiry young man said.

Mason grabbed the documents and shoved them into his bag. "I'll review these over lunch and will release you from your subpoena obligations if everything is here."

All three of them nodded.

"Do we need to come back?" the stout woman said.

"Tell you what," Mason said. "If everything is in order, you don't have to plan to come back. But if I find that anything is missing, I'll call you to come back over. Fair?"

They all nodded. Then, they turned and headed out of the courthouse.

Stepping through the gate, an attractive woman rose from the closest pew. Lexi met Mason's eyes, then she moved towards him as he stepped through the gate.

"I appreciate your coming by and supporting Tyler," Mason said.

"Shouldn't you have introduced me to the jury?" Lexi snapped.

Mason continued walking, headed towards the door. "We don't have a lot of time."

Tyler and Lexi trailed after him, as Mason moved along to the waiting area outside of the courtroom. He stepped through a set of double doors, then walked across a large upper lobby area. Mason descended a spiral staircase to the lobby.

Outside, he turned to Lexi and waited for her to settle down. She stood there fidgeting and avoiding eye contact.

"I really do not have time to explain strategy considerations," Mason said. "And even if I did have the time, which I don't, I couldn't speak to you about my strategy and impressions because all of that is subject to attorney/client privilege."

"But I'm his girlfriend," Lexi said. "Live-in girlfriend."

Tyler looked like he wanted to jump in and take her side.

Mason held up a hand, cautioning Tyler from speaking. "I understand this is difficult," Mason said, trying to mollify her. "But anything that we say in front of you could be used against Tyler. The prosecution could call you as a witness and ask you about our discussions. So, while my approach may appear harsh, it comes with good reasons."

Lexi nodded. "Understood."

"We are going to head over to my office," Mason said. "Tyler and I will order lunch in and review for our next steps. I can recommend a few places for you to eat."

"No. That's okay." Lexi reached into her pocket and pulled out a pack of smokes.

"You sure."

"Absolutely," she said. "I know the town."

"Suit yourself," Mason said, stepping away.

Tyler leaned over and gave Lexi a kiss on the cheek. She really didn't respond affectionately.

Mason waited for the kid to catch up.

As soon as Tyler turned away from his girlfriend, she

reached into her coat and pulled out her cellphone.

Mason wondered if she was just checking messages or social media while killing time having a smoke. It also crossed his mind that she might be reaching out to someone. He wondered who Lexi might be contacting.

The police? Mason thought.

CHAPTER THIRTY-SIX

WADE GARRETT was pleased to see a call come in from Lexi. The judge had ordered that all witnesses be sequestered, and the prosecution had listed him as a potential witness.

He couldn't unwind and needed something to take his mind off the trial.

Wade drove his truck around to the back of the courthouse parking lot. Lexi climbed in and gave him a passionate kiss. Her tongue swirled around in his mouth in a manner Crystal hadn't done in a long time.

"You up for a quickie?" he said.

"Here?" she questioned.

Her response wasn't a no; she hadn't declined. Wade grinned, wondering if he could get her to mount him in the parking lot where cops and judges were just a stone's throw away.

"That would be nice," Wade said, shifting into drive.

"Not sure it's the best idea right now."

"Me either."

Wade drove through the parking lot and meandered through a few city streets, until he came to a parking garage located a few blocks off Main Street. He circled the garage moving upwards until the number of vehicles became sparse.

Then he found an isolated spot off to the side.

As soon as he moved out from under the steering wheel, he felt her hand cup his privates. They unbuttoned each other's jeans, then she pulled hers down. Lexi wriggled and wormed out of the jeans and her thong pulled off along with them.

She climbed on him and the two of them went at it like wildcats.

Their random hookup was over soon after it started, but she appeared to be satisfied. Wade had a way of making a woman glad to be with him, even when it was mostly about him.

After straightening up, the two of them headed over to a popular restaurant and found a quiet spot in a booth. The place had a sprawling bar that wrapped around a large space. It was covered by a marble top. High ceilings and worn tile flooring accented the massive picture windows overlooking Main Street. The building had once housed the local exchange and retained some of its historic charm, with plank floors in areas and intricate woodwork.

There was an area to the side of the bar that housed tanks and vats for brewing beer.

Lexi ordered a soft drink and Wade asked for a craft beer. He wasn't planning to testify that day. They put in orders, then he looked across at her.

"I'm not sure this is the best idea," Lexi said.

"What?" Wade didn't quite follow.

"The two of us being seen together... with everything that's going down."

"I'm just sitting here having a bite with my business partner's girlfriend, while he's going through a tough time." Wade cracked a reassuring grin.

She seemed relieved by his comment. "You sure know how to put a girl at ease."

"I've always said that if you act natural, nobody will suspect anything."

The server brought over their drinks and set them down on the table then he left. Lexi took a sip and played with her straw.

"Are we all set, then?" asked Wade.

"Sure."

"Can you tell me what's going on over there?" Wade asked.

Lexi looked at him suspiciously. "Not much."

"What have the cops said?"

Lexi shook her head. "Nothing."

Wade furrowed his eyebrows in disbelief.

"They've only selected the jury."

"Really?" Wade said. "That's it. They've been at it all day."

"Well, that's all they've done."

The sever came by and placed a hamburger and fries in front of Wade and a cobb salad in before Lexi. He made sure they didn't need anything else, then he moved on to the next table.

Wade dug into his meal like he hadn't eaten in two weeks.

"You sure are hungry," Lexi said.

"Maybe you got my appetite up," Wade said, grinning.

She picked at her salad and appeared distracted.

"Did something go down over there," Wade said. "Something that got you distracted."

"Maybe," she said. "I'm not sure."

"Well, you can tell me what's up," Wade said.

"Tyler has this lawyer that seems like a country bumpkin," Lexi said. "But I'm not so sure about him."

"Meaning?"

"He might be smarter than he lets on."

"Probably a good way to go about handling a criminal defense case," Wade said. "Worked well for Columbo."

"Anyway, he might know more than people think."

"I'm sure he does. A lawyer like that ain't going to reveal everything he's thinking."

"There's something more," Lexi added.

"What?"

"He's requested documents from different businesses and such."

"Like what?" Wade bellowed.

"Don't yell at me," Lexi said, curling up.

Wade watched her pull her arms together, wrapping them around her torso, like a baby snuggling in a crib. She'd clearly been through some abuse at one point. He needed to calm down, tease the information from her. "I'm sorry," he said, soothingly.

"Just don't need to be hollered at."

"I know. This situation has me all nerved up."

"You ain't the only one."

She ate some of her salad and took a drink. Then, she pushed her food around the salad bowl, without digging in.

"What kind of documents?" Wade said.

Lexi shrugged. "Don't know."

"How do you know about them?"

"It came up."

"What did they say?"

"The lawyer said there were documents from entities, and he planned to use them to impeach people. I thought you could only do that to a president."

Impeach, Wade thought.

"Anyway. It's got me worried."

"Why?"

"Maybe there's something in there about us."

Something about us, Wade considered. *Something about me is more like it.*

The very thought of it made his blood boil. Wade wanted to clock somebody, like that frigging lawyer. Then, he realized that Lexi was staring at him, frightened. She'd slid against the back of the booth, as though she was scared to death of him.

Good. Be afraid. Wade smirked. *They all should be scared.*

Wade didn't plan to let some wussy like Tyler ruin him, either.

CHAPTER THIRTY-SEVEN

MASON returned to the courtroom after lunch and found the gallery packed with spectators. Members of the press probably wanted to hear opening statements to get a preview of the evidence.

Sam Makinson was seated in the middle of the first row behind the prosecution table, which was situated closer to the jury box. Kyle Wentworth sat further back near the aisle. He nodded to Mason as the defense lawyer and his client walked past.

The prosecutors were huddled at their table, scratching out last minute thoughts on notepads before they launched their opening salvo.

Swinging the gate open, Mason stepped through and held it for Tyler. The kid seemed more nervous than before. The crowd had likely thrown him for a loop. Mason was relieved that Tyler wouldn't testify for at least a couple of days, if at all.

Mason reached his table and the door in the back of the courtroom swung open. The judge took the bench before Mason could even unpack.

The bailiff called for everyone to stand.

Once the judge was seated, he looked towards the gallery. "You may be seated."

People in the gallery sat down, but the lawyers knew to remaining standing. Tyler followed Mason's lead. The attorneys waited for the judge to cue them on what to do.

"We'll bring the jury in and get started," Judge Wakefield said.

The bailiff called, "All rise for the jury."

Everyone in the gallery stood back up.

Another bailiff opened a door to the rear of the courtroom and the jury filed in.

The jurors got situated in their seats in the jury box, then the bailiffs turned and faced the judge. Judge Wakefield told everyone in the courtroom they could be seated.

Mason watched the jurors out of the corner of his eye. The one in the front closest to the witness box was a bit of a concern. A nurse who had appeared to be enthralled with Cody Harper; she would likely give a lot of weight to the state's witnesses.

He checked the others that he thought might be more favorable to the defense. A local mechanic sat in the back. There was a real estate agent who ran his own business in the back row farthest from the witness box. And a guy that ran a snowplow business in the front, who was seated next to a young female college student. The rest were people that could go either way, including a hospital administrator, a financial planner, a woman who worked in a coin store, and the rest who were employed with various local small businesses.

One of the alternates was married to a police officer, so Mason hadn't taken any chances in striking one of the jurors out of fear it could have led to more challenges, which would have moved her up to being on the jury. He planned to object to allowing the alternates to deliberate.

Judge Wakefield looked at Harper. "Ready to get started?"

"Yes, Your Honor," Harper said, rising from his chair.

He casually walked in front of the jury, obviously comfortable in a courtroom.

Mason had tried civil cases against lawyers that weren't accustomed to trying cases in front of a jury. Such lawyers often pulled out the podium and hid behind it. They piled binders full of documents and notepads onto the podium, then they read their opening statements almost verbatim from a sheet of paper.

Cody Harper stood in front of the jury without anything in his hands. He'd moved the podium out of the way before things had gotten started for the afternoon session. It was over by a corner of the jury box, ready for use during witness examinations.

Harper took a moment to scan the jury box and smiled at everyone. Most of the jurors sat before him looking stone-faced, less enthralled with his boyish good looks than they had been that morning.

"As I mentioned previously, I am Cody Harper." He pointed at his colleague. "With me today is Susan Atkins."

Several jurors looked over at the young woman and nodded with approval.

"We are with the Attorney General's Office in Concord," Harper said. "I plan to keep this relatively short today."

A few jurors smiled, likely recalling the extensive grilling he'd dragged them through.

"This matter involves a serious crime." Harper pointed at a few people seated in the pews behind the prosecutor's table. "Also with me today are members of the victim's family."

They were located between Makinson and the aisle. All of them looked grim.

"This matter involves four people getting into dire financial circumstances," Harper said. "The defendant, Tyler Cummings, was one of those four business partners. The evidence will show that they bought a factory out in Wilton and had a mortgage on the building. They also owed monies to the prior building owner through a private loan."

Harper paused and looked each juror in the eyes, making sure that the complex backdrop had sunk in.

"After falling behind on their obligations, the partners tried to work things out with the prior business owner, Herbert Jenkins."

Again, Harper paused for dramatic effect.

"Jenkins wouldn't agree to a workout without security, and

the partners didn't have security. Now, this is where things got out of hand."

The prosecutor had set them up for a dramatic statement, and the jury took it hook, line and sinker. They all sat up and paid close attention.

"Wade Garrett had mentioned burning the mill down for the insurance money. He was only half serious when he made the statement, but it planted a seed in Tyler Cummings' head. The defendant ruminated about the idea of arson. It was a way out."

A few jurors had skeptical looks on their faces.

"After the deal didn't work out with Jenkins, the defendant left the office of the mill building. He waited in the parking lot. When Jenkins came out, the defendant confronted Jenkins. They had an argument and the onery old man got the better of the defendant. The defendant was enraged, and he pulled out a .25 caliber pistol and fired it at the old man, hitting him in the head."

Most of the jury sat there in shock. A couple looked over at Tyler and scowled.

"The bullet entered the victim's head and killed him. Strangely, as it happens at times, the gunshot wound did not cause a lot of blood loss. The defendant dragged the victim back into the building through a basement door. There is evidence that the victim was not dead at the time he was dragged into the building, and so the defendant took the victim by force, unwillingly. The defendant tossed the victim on the floor near a stairwell. Then he went back to his truck and grabbed a couple of gas cans."

The story was compelling, but it lacked mention of eyewitnesses. A few jurors still seemed to question it.

"The defendant had some early training as an electrician's apprentice during high school and college. He played around with the wiring in the basement and poured gas in a few locations. Then he torched the place, hoping we'd think the victim died of smoke inhalation, which is what we initially thought."

Harper paused. Then he moved a little closer to the jury box.

"You will hear ample evidence to return a verdict in this matter," Harper said. "At the close of this matter, we are going to ask you to find the defendant guilty of capital murder, which means that a murder took place when somebody was kidnapped, or held hostage. We also will ask you to find the defendant guilty of arson."

Cody Harper flashed a quick, professional smile. Then he turned away and walked back to the prosecution table and sat down. He'd done a splendid presentation.

***

MASON spent the lunch break at his office reviewing the documents he'd received from subpoenas. Diane had ordered sandwiches, so he and Tyler ate lunch in the conference room while seated at the oak library table.

He had drafted an outline for an opening statement on a notepad. It had bullet points for the items he wanted to cover. Hearing the prosecution's opening, Mason planned to jettison his outline.

After returning to court, Judge Wakefield looked at Mason. "Your turn."

Mason stood up. "Thank you, Your Honor."

Scooting between the two counsel tables, Mason walked into the well of the courtroom. He took a position before the jury box.

"I'm Mason Walters," he said. "I'm a local attorney who represents the defendant in this matter." He pointed at the defendant. "I'm here with Tyler Cummings."

Several jurors looked over at the defendant. A few didn't seem to like him.

"We thank you for your time and consideration," Mason said. "I know that a trial can be demanding on you and your family members, so we appreciate your service."

All the jurors nodded with appreciation.

"An opening statement is a time when the attorneys stand

before you and explain what the evidence will show. Then during the trial, the parties put evidence before you. It comes in as testimony and as exhibits."

Everyone on the jury appeared interested in how a trial worked.

"After the close of evidence, the lawyers come back here and make arguments." Mason moved a little closer. "Argument isn't evidence."

He stepped back and let that sit.

"The judge will then instruct you on the law. Then you'll go back and deliberate."

"So, let's handle this part," Mason said. "What will the evidence show?"

He sounded like a person visiting school children, telling them about his career.

"You heard a great story," Mason said. "What about the evidence?"

He moved closer and looked them over, trying to pique their interest. It seemed to work.

"Our evidence in this case is a gas can," Mason said. "That's right. A gas can."

Mason scanned the jury box. Some jurors looked confused. A few others looked pissed off, like maybe they felt they had been duped. The mechanic glanced over at Cody Harper and scowled.

"At no time did Tyler Cummings say he was going to commit arson," Mason continued. "The police found a gas can at the scene with the defendant's fingerprints on it. You'll hear testimony that the police took a similar can from an unlocked barn."

Mason stepped closer and lowered his voice. "Anyone could have taken that can."

"There's no murder weapon," Mason said. "There isn't an eyewitness."

Some jurors looked even more confused. Others seemed to run everything they had heard through their minds. Mason's goal during voir dire was to get them to commit to being objective until they heard the entire case. Now, he was showing them that there were two sides to the story.

Mason paced before the jury, as though considering what to say next. Many of the jurors traced his movements around the courtroom. He turned and faced them.

"There were others with motive and opportunity," Mason finally said. Then, he walked back to his table.

Mason glanced at Tyler. The young man looked dismayed. More than unsettled; there was a hint of anger in his eyes.

The kid thinks he's been set up, Mason thought.

CHAPTER THIRTY-EIGHT

MASON took a seat in an oak chair and waited to see what Cody Harper would do next.

"Mr. Harper," Judge Wakefield said. "You may call your first witness."

Harper stood up looking like a deer staring at headlights. "Uh..."

"What is it?" the judge asked.

"Your, Honor," Harper stammered. "We didn't expect openings to go so quickly."

"Are you telling me that you don't have a witness ready?" Judge Wakefield chided him.

"We might need a minute," Harper said, turning around and facing a group of police and support personnel from his office, located in the pews behind the prosecution table.

"Mr. Harper," Judge Wakefield said. "We like to run an efficient courtroom. I don't like to waste time. Let's go ahead and take our afternoon break. Please don't let this happen again."

"Thank you, Your Honor," Harper said.

The judge excused the jury and left the bench.

Mason finally had an opportunity to open his trial bag. He leaned over, trying to catch part of the discussion at the next table. They were talking about getting a detective over from Milford, but Sam Makinson came forward and whispered to Harper.

The dilemma was going to cause Harper to take witnesses out of order.

Mason told Tyler to stretch out and use the facilities, while he remained at counsel table reviewing the documents he'd received that morning.

***

LATER, the court had reconvened after the break and Cody Harper stood at his table waiting for the judge to address him. The jury watched with indifference.

"The State calls Scott Bancroft," Harper said.

I knew it, Mason thought.

The courtroom doors opened, and a police officer walked in with a person trailing slightly beside him. Scott Bancroft was the consummate salesperson. He wore an expensive suit and tie, and his hair was slicked back like he was ready to wheel and deal.

Bancroft strutted back to the witness box and sat down, looking like he didn't have a care in the world. Mason figured that Makinson had gotten Bancroft a sweet deal with full immunity.

After he was sworn in, Harper walked over to the podium located at the edge of the jury box. He placed a stack of documents on the podium. Then he set a cup of water on the top edge of the lectern.

Harper spent some time going over Bancroft's education and employment history. The man had grown up in the area, gone to Keene State College and majored in business. He worked in various sales positions, including a period of time where he'd been employed in a family business. He'd bought into the Wilco Manufacturing Company in order to branch out on his own.

Next, the able prosecutor had Bancroft walk through the financial arrangements, including the bank loan, note to Jenkins, as well as the life insurance policy on Jenkins. Then they went over the financial issues.

"What did you try to do relative to this financial situation?"

Harper asked.

"The first thing was to try and talk to Jenkins about a workout," Bancroft said.

"Can you describe how that transpired?"

"About two weeks before the fire, Jenkins met us at the office. He said that he was willing to engage in a workout, but only if my father provided security going forward."

"Was that something the partners wanted to do?" Harper said.

"The partners all wanted to enter a workout." Bancroft looked at the jury and tried to impress them. "Some kind of arrangement where you pay less than the amount owed for a period of time, with the payment amounts being increased later."

A few jurors nodded, as if appreciating the explanation.

"Did you enter a workout?" Harper asked.

Bancroft shook his head. "No."

"Why not?"

"I had told Wade and Tyler that my father wasn't in a position to provide security." Bancroft looked at the jury again. "He was hurting like a lot of other businesses."

"What happened during the meeting?"

"The meeting ended with Jenkins promising to come back and talk further."

"Did you think you could deliver security when that meeting terminated?" Harper said.

"No." Bancroft forced a smile. "I'd told Wade it couldn't be done."

"What happened from there?"

"Wade and Tyler wanted more time," Bancroft said.

"Do you know why?"

Bancroft shrugged. "I didn't get it. Figured they…"

"Objection!" Mason called out.

"Basis?" Judge Wakefield asked.

"Speculation."

"The objection is sustained."

"Do you have knowledge of whether the partners devised any plans?" Harper said.

"Yes."

"What were the plans?"

"Wade and Tyler wanted to torch the place if they couldn't work things out with Jenkins," Bancroft said.

"Did they make any definitive plans?"

"Not to my knowledge." Bancroft turned to the jury. "I thought that it was just talk when it first came up. It wasn't something I thought would ever happen."

"Were you privy to any further planning about burning the building?"

Bancroft shook his head. "No. It never came up again."

"Did you have another meeting with Jenkins?"

"Yes."

"What happened?"

"Jenkins met with three of us at the office in the mill." Bancroft looked over at the jury. "Our other partner, Crystal, didn't have anything to do with these meetings."

"Try to answer the question," Judge Wakefield said.

"Sure," Bancroft said, apologetically.

"You may continue," Harper said.

"Like I was saying," Bancroft said. "Jenkins showed up. We offered a workout. He wouldn't take anything without security."

"Then what happened?"

"Jenkins and Wade got into a heated argument," Bancroft said. "Then a funny thing happened…"

"Please tell us," Harper said, flashing his politician's smile.

"Tyler had been fairly quiet during both meetings. But he suddenly got angry and stormed out of the office. Then Jenkins took off right afterwards."

"What happened from there?"

"I had some words with Wade, explaining how my father couldn't provide security."

"What happened next?"

"I'd had it for the day." Bancroft sounded aloof.

"And?"

"Well, I left the mill. Got into my truck and drove home."

Harper turned to the judge and waited. Judge Wakefield was taking down notes and took a moment to register the sudden end to the questioning.

"Yes?" Judge Wakefield said.

"I've completed my examination of this witness at this time," Harper said.

"Very well," Judge Wakefield said.

Harper walked over to his table and sat down. A satisfied grin was plastered on his face.

Mason understood the inference and could already hear Harper's closing argument. *Tyler was the last person to see Jenkins alive.*

CHAPTER THIRTY-NINE

THE JUDGE called a recess for the day and reminded Bancroft that he remained under oath. Then the jury was excused, and the judge left the bench.

Mason packed up and walked out of the courthouse with Tyler by his side.

He could tell the kid wanted to head over to the office, but Mason had things to do to prepare for the following day. Many clients didn't understand that their role was to testify and present well at counsel table. During the throes of a trial, there wasn't time to kick around ideas and strategy points for the sake of placating the client.

They stood on the sidewalk outside the courthouse. Flags rattled a loose rope on the flagpole and wind blew through the open space.

"How do you think it went today?" Tyler asked.

"We selected a decent jury," Mason said. "It wasn't ideal for a criminal defense case, but we avoided people in law enforcement and the legal profession, and engineers."

"What about the rest of it?" Tyler said.

"The prosecution opened well. We did a decent opening, too."

"How about Scott Bancroft?"

"Well, his testimony isn't over. He set up several points, but the financial issues could point to any of them."

"Did they score any points?"

"Perhaps."

"Like what?"

"Bancroft makes it sound like you were the last one to see Jenkins alive."

Tyler considered the comment. "I hadn't picked up on that. But wouldn't the killer be the one to have seen him last?"

Mason looked into the young man's naïve eyes. "You would think so."

"What are we going to do now?" asked Tyler.

"There's a lot to do to prepare for tomorrow. I really don't have time to chat."

"Understood," Tyler said. "You've got work to do."

"I'll see you here about 8:30 AM," Mason said.

"Will do."

Mason clapped the kid on the shoulder. Tyler smiled, then he turned and headed down the sidewalk leading out back to a parking lot.

The lawyer went in the other direction. Mason lugged his trial bag a few city blocks, then he carried it up a flight of stairs to his office. Diane had gone for the day.

He walked into the conference room and set the trial bag on an old courthouse chair.

Fishing through the various documents, he reorganized everything and removed items that were no longer needed, like the outline to his opening statement. Once the bag was all set, he checked for messages and emails.

Then, he packed up for the night and headed home.

Mason encountered light traffic and quickly arrived at his house.

After parking in the carriage shed, he walked across the gravel driveway and entered a warm house. Benny pattered over the plank floor, and Mason gave the dog a pat on the head.

Mason hung his wool overcoat on a peg. Then, he headed into a room in the front of the house that was used for a study. Benny trailed after him. He set the trial bag on the floor. Then, he removed his suit coat and draped it across a captain's chair, which was embossed with the UNH school logo.

He sat down on the sofa and removed his dress shoes.

Taking a moment to catch his breath, he decided that he was getting too old for murder trials. High stakes litigation was draining. He tucked his tie inside his shirt to avoid getting it stained from dinner.

Then, Mason got up and headed into the kitchen.

He found Amelia busy at the stove. The gourmet kitchen was lit up and bustling with activity. Buzzers were beeping and a pan sizzled on the stove.

"That smells delicious," he said. "What are you making?"

"Smothered chicken," Amelia said, smiling.

Mason thought about the meal. It was chicken breasts made with onions, bacon, and gravy on top. He walked over to the refrigerator and opened the stainless-steel door. The partial bottle of Barolo was in the door bin.

He started to reach for the neck of the bottle. Then, he thought better of it.

"Not going to finish that off tonight?" she said.

Mason shook his head. "Afraid I need something a bit stronger."

He trundled off to the dining room and approached the antique liquor cabinet. Pulling the handle on a swinging door, he opened the cabinet and grabbed a bottle of Booker's Bourbon. He reached for an old-fashioned glass off the interior shelf. It was etched with a dry fly on the glass.

Returning to the kitchen, he fetched a couple of oversized ice cubes from the freezer. He cracked them on the soapstone countertop with a mallet, breaking the ice into pieces.

Then, he brushed the shards into his glass and poured two fingers of bourbon.

Mason took a sip and the cocktail was divine.

"Went that well today?" Amelia asked, sarcastically.

"Just the opposite," Mason replied.

"Then what's got you all in a tizzy?"

Mason took another sip of his drink. Then, he glanced over at his wife and broke one of his cardinal rules in not talking about a case. "The kid's probably innocent."

CHAPTER FORTY

THE NEXT morning, the entrance to the courthouse was busier than usual. It took Mason a while to get through security.

When he finally got upstairs and entered the courtroom, Mason found the gallery packed with spectators. He headed through the gate and was surprised to learn that Tyler wasn't present in the courthouse.

Mason unpacked his trial bag, then he glanced around the room.

The prosecutors were busy scribbling on notepads. Scott Bancroft stood inside the rail alongside the pews behind the prosecution table. He was talking to Sam Makinson. Seated beside the famed lawyer was Kyle Wentworth.

Kyle was smiling and participating in a jovial discussion. Suddenly, he and Makinson were chummy companions. This wouldn't bode well for Tyler.

The courtroom doors swung open, and Tyler entered. He walked towards the gate looking worried. The kid was running late to one of the most important events in his adult life. Just as he reached the gate, a door in the back of the courtroom opened and the judge took the bench.

Another door opened and the jury filed in.

A bailiff called out, "All rise."

Mason stood up behind the defense table, and Tyler came to attention. The kid held the gate open and waited for an opportunity to break towards the defense table.

"You may be seated," Judge Wakefield said.

Tyler rushed over and took a seat beside Mason.

Mason wished the kid had acted more casual. All he managed to accomplish was attracting attention to himself. A few jurors saw him stumble over to the table.

"You may cross-examine the witness," the judge said to Mason.

Mason stood up and waited for Bancroft to approach the witness box.

When the witness stepped up to the witnesses stand, the judge turned and addressed him. "You are still under oath."

"Yes, sir," Bancroft said, then he sat down.

Mason walked over to the podium and set a stack of documents down. "Good morning, Mr. Bancroft," Mason said.

Bancroft smirked at Mason. "Good morning to you."

Mason got the feeling the slick salesman intended to spar with him.

"You testified on behalf of the prosecution, correct?" asked Mason.

"I was asked to give testimony and I came here and told the truth."

"You were a witness for the prosecution, right?"

"I wouldn't call it that. More of an independent witness," Bancroft said, grinning.

"Were you promised anything for your testimony?"

"I'm not sure what you mean,' Bancroft said.

"Did you get charged with any crimes related to the fire at the mill?"

"Yes."

"What was the charge?"

"They charged me with conspiracy to commit arson," Bancroft said, hanging his head low.

"Did that charge get resolved?"

"Sort of," Bancroft said. "It was continued without a finding."

"What's your understanding of the status of that charge?"

"The charge will not be prosecuted, and if I remain on good behavior and do not commit a similar offense, it will be dismissed within a year." Bancroft turned to the jury. "See it's sort of to protect the public."

"It's to protect the public?" Mason said.

"Yes. Keeps a person on the straight and narrow."

"You testified that *all* the partners were in financial trouble, right?"

"I guess you can say that."

Mason stepped away from the lectern and moved closer to the witness. "You never saw Tyler do anything in furtherance of committing arson on the mill, right?"

"I guess you can say that, too."

"You said that Tyler left the second meeting before Jenkins, right?"

"Yeah. That's what I said."

"And you left the mill after Jenkins, right?"

"Yes. That's what I said," Bancroft said.

"You didn't see either Tyler or Jenkins in the parking lot?" Mason's tone reflected suspicion.

"Yeah. That's right."

"Wade Garrett hadn't left the building to your knowledge?"

"He was there when I left."

"What was he doing?"

"Just standing in the office."

Mason moved into the well of the courtroom, closer to the witness. "You're aware that Wade was down in the basement working on equipment after you left for the evening, right?"

"Well, I've heard that, but—"

"Objection!" Harper bellowed.

"Sustained," Judge Wakefield said.

"You didn't see Mr. Cummings shoot anyone, right?"

"No, sir."

"You didn't see him start a fire?"

"No, sir."

"You didn't see him play around with any wiring?"

"No, sir," Bancroft said. "If I had seen him doing it, I'd have told him to stop."

"Objection," Mason said, turning to the judge. "The last part was nonresponsive. The defense moves to strike it."

"Sustained," said Judge Wakefield.

Harper was half out of his chair when the judge ruled on the objection.

The judge looked at the jury. "You will disregard that last comment from the witness." The judge looked at Bancroft. "And you will just answer the questions asked. I don't want to be here into next week. If the prosecutor wants to follow up, he has an opportunity to do so."

"Understood," Bancroft said to the judge.

"Wade Garrett performs repair work on the equipment, right?" Mason said.

"Yes. He's handy that way."

"You don't know where Wade Garrett was located at the time Mr. Jenkins was shot, right?"

"No. I do not."

"You don't know where Wade Garrett was at the time the fire started, correct?"

"That is correct."

Mason walked right up to the witness box and stood a few feet away. "Isn't it true that Wade Garrett owns a Beretta .25 caliber pistol?" Mason asked.

"Objection!" Harper griped.

Judge Wakefield shook his head, annoyed. "The witness can answer if he knows."

"I'm not sure," Bancroft said. "But I think so."

"Move to strike," Harper said.

Judge Wakefield looked at Mason. "Counselor?"

"Let me ask the basis of his knowledge."

"Go ahead."

"Why do you think so?"

Bancroft seemed to mull the question over. "A year ago, Wade took me to a shooting range. He had a deer rifle he was sighting in. Pretty sure we took some shots with the Beretta, too."

Mason walked back to the podium and considered next

steps. He had a stack of documents showing the debt of the Bancroft family. He'd planned to point blame at Wade and the Bancrofts, but things had turned out nicely with this examination.

"I've concluded my examination of this witness," Mason said to the judge.

Judge Wakefield looked at Harper. "Any redirect?"

Harper and his second chair counsel whispered. Then, Harper shook his head. "No, Your Honor."

CHAPTER FORTY-ONE

THE JUDGE jotted down a few notes, then he looked at Harper. "You may call your next witness."

Harper called Detective Sergeant LeClair to the stand.

Murder cases in New Hampshire typically involve a detective from the State Police leading the investigation. That detective is often the key witness at trial. But this case initially seemed like an accidental death, or a death caused from smoke inhalation, so the State Police were called in later.

LeClair described her role in serving as a liaison with the Wilton Police Department. Her main role was to describe the gas can found at the scene, and the fingerprints on the fuel can matching the prints taken from the defendant when he was booked. She also provided cover for the initial arrest for felony murder and gave chain of custody testimony for the evidence gathered at the scene, and Tyler's house.

Mason merely cross-examined her by eliciting testimony about how the matching gas can was found in an unlocked barn. He went through a standard list of questions about how Tyler Cummings didn't own a gun, wasn't seen lighting a fire, and how there weren't any witnesses to a murder.

The next witness was a crime scene officer from the State Police. He testified about the technical aspects of the fire patterns and the fingerprint evidence. Mason crossed-examined him the same way.

Another detective for the State Police testified about research done into the defendant's background as an apprentice to an electrician back in Wisconsin. Mason tried to object based upon hearsay, but the judge let the testimony in under a business records exception, where the officer had obtained a journeyman's license history.

Mason then moved into the well of the courtroom. "Mr. Jenkins died from a .25 caliber gunshot wound to the head, right?"

"Yes, I believe so."

"That could have been a .25 caliber Beretta semi-automatic, correct?"

"We do not know the make or model because the weapon was never located."

"But it's possible that it could have been a .25 caliber Beretta?"

"Yes. That is possible."

"Did you ever investigate to see if Wade Garrett owned a .25 caliber pistol?" Mason said.

The detective looked stumped. "We searched his house. And we searched his person. But we did not locate a .25 caliber pistol, and we didn't find any records related to one."

"Did you search his safety deposit box at the local bank?"

"Sir?" The detective looked confused and worried.

"Well, did you?"

"We were not aware of a safety deposit box."

Mason walked over to the podium and grabbed a sheet of paper. "Did you check the local gun stores for transactions on a .25 caliber pistol?"

"Yes, but—"

"Thank you," Mason said. "You answered the question."

Harper started to rise from his chair to object. Then he sat back down.

"You looked at records from the local gun stores, right?"

"We did."

Mason looked at the judge. "May I approach?"

"You may."

Mason walked over to the witness box and placed a document on the ledge. "Please take a look at the document and see if it refreshes your recollection of Wade Garrett purchasing a .25 caliber pistol."

The detective looked at the document. Then, he shook his head. "Afraid that it doesn't."

Mason smiled, like he was expecting such a response. It really didn't matter, the jury now understood that Mason had supporting documentation to show that Garrett owned the type of pistol used to kill Jenkins.

He retrieved the document, then he faced the judge. "I've concluded my examination of this witness."

"Any redirect?" Judge Wakefield asked Harper.

Cody Harper shook his head, apparently disgusted in the missteps by the police.

CHAPTER FORTY-TWO

AFTER the lunch break, the prosecution called its private expert, who opined that the fire was a result of arson. He testified about the use of accelerants, and the multiple points of origin. The expert also provided testimony about how fuses were removed, and a few breakers had been flipped off.

Mason followed the similar pattern in cross-examining the witnesses. He hit home the points that nobody saw the defendant commit either crime. With this witness, Mason kept the examination short in order to avoid alienating the jury with repetitive questions. However, he layered enough repetition into his cross-examinations to cement the major points for the jury. Mason simply didn't want those points getting lost during deliberations.

When he finished his examination of the expert, Mason noticed that Lexi had finally shown up for trial. He wondered where she had been, but he figured that work or another commitment had gotten in the way.

Now that she was seated in the gallery, his concern hadn't waned. Lexi was seated snug beside a man in a trucker's jacket.

***

WADE GARRETT had been sequestered during the other witness testimony. But he'd ventured into the courtroom during the expert's cross-examination.

Kyle Wentworth had told him to appear at precisely 2:00 PM, so he'd done so.

Wade knew Kyle had wanted him to wait out in the hallway.

But there wasn't anyone out there and the waiting had gotten boring. He figured it couldn't cause any harm. He was there to tell the truth.

Leaning over towards Lexi, he said, "Did I miss anything?"

"Yeah," Lexi said.

"They were talking about a gun when I got in here."

"A gun?" Wade said. "What gun?"

"*Your* gun," she said.

Wade thought about the pistol in the glove box of his truck, parked in the courthouse lot right outside the building. His pulse quickened. He wanted to get up and run.

Then, he heard his name mentioned.

Cody Harper had just called him to the stand. Wade slipped out of his coat and headed for the gate.

CHAPTER FORTY-THREE

MASON watched Wade Garrett approach the witness stand. The guy was usually sure of himself and quite cocky. But he moved slowly and appeared guarded.

Once he was sworn in, Harper walked into the well of the courtroom. "I'm just going to ask you a few questions Mr. Garrett," Harper said.

"Shoot," Wade responded.

A few members of the jury frowned at the use of the expression during a murder trial.

"Can you describe the financial condition of your business at the time of the events subject to this legal matter?" asked Harper.

"Sure. We was hurtin' and orders had slowed down."

"What did that mean financially?"

"It meant that we were behind on our loan to the bank and on payments to Herbert Jenkins," Wade said. "Orders being down meant that receivables would drop, making matters worse."

"Did you want to work things out with Jenkins?"

"Most definitely. I wanted to frame a workout, so we could keep going."

"What did you want to do?" Harper said.

"I offered Jenkins a workout," Wade said. "It would help everyone involved, actually."

"Why is that?"

"See," Wade said, speaking to Harper. "If Jenkins called in his note, he'd be stuck with the mill, all the expenses to maintain it, and he wouldn't have any money coming in. A workout would keep money coming in, and it would avoid him taking over expenses like electricity, heat, property taxes and insurance."

"Was there any reason why you didn't accomplish a workout?" Harper said.

"Jenkins wanted security. And Scott Bancroft was too chickenshit to talk to his father."

Harper appeared to notice that Wade Garrett was fired up.

Moving over to the podium, Harper paused his examination. It was clearly meant to allow Garrett time to cool off. "Tell us how the second meeting concluded?"

"It was weird," Wade said. "The discussion seemed to reach an impasse. All of a sudden Tyler bolted from the office. Then Jenkins left."

"Had you ever mentioned arson?" Harper asked.

Wade paused, as if sensing he might be walking into a trap. "Not exactly."

"Tell us what you said."

"I said that if we couldn't get a workout with Jenkins, we could torch the place."

People in the gallery gasped at the admission.

"Did you plan to commit arson."

"Hell, no."

"What was your plan?"

"Nothing," Wade protested. "I figured we still had a shot at a workout. Then that little sucker went ahead and burned my business down."

Wade stared at Tyler like he wanted to kill the kid.

"Can you tell us what happened from there?" Harper said.

"I went to work on some equipment in order to take my mind off things," Garrett said. "I was in the storage room putting some tools away when smoke seeped under the door. I stepped out of the room and found the mill was ablaze."

"Did you encounter Jenkins after he stormed out of the

mill?"

"No, sir," Wade said, staring Harper in the eyes. "I most certainly did not."

Harper completed his examination. Once again, he sought to leave the jury with the notion that Tyler was likely the last person to see Jenkins alive.

**

MASON stood up and walked over to the podium. Wade Garrett eyed him every step of the way, appearing like a pot simmering to a boil.

Mason set a cup of water down on the lectern, then he placed a stack of documents in the center of the podium. He glanced up at Wade as he took his time getting ready for his examination.

Taking a sip of water, Mason delayed the process further.

Wade looked like he was ready to snap. The suspense was building, and the witness was trapped on the stand, like a castaway on an island, alone and afraid.

"You were in just as much of a financial pickle as Tyler Cummings, right?" Mason asked.

"If all this hadn't of happened, we probably could have entered a workout."

"You're certain of that?" Mason said.

"Pretty much."

"You were the first one to mention torching the place, right?"

Wade hesitated. "I guess you can say that's true."

"You were the only one who had mentioned arson, right?" Mason said.

Mason glanced over and noticed that Harper looked worried about the question. The prosecutor didn't know the answer, and he had put Bancroft on the stand saying that Tyler had mentioned it too.

"It came up the one time. I'm not certain if anyone else said anything."

Harper looked relieved by the answer.

Mason moved away from the podium into the well of the courtroom. "Did you get any favorable treatment from the prosecution for your testimony?"

"Like a plea deal?" Wade said.

"Yes. Like a plea deal?"

"Nope." Wade shook his head. "The prosecutor, Mr. Harper, asked me to come in here and tell the truth. He said that if I'm honest, then they'll consider it when they review my case further."

"So, there were no promises?"

"Nothing in writing."

"What did they say would happen with your case?"

"That it might be continued without a finding," Wade muttered.

Mason moved a little closer to the witness stand.

"You own a .25 caliber pistol, right?" Mason said.

"Guess you already know the answer."

Judge Wakefield turned to the witness. "Please answer the question."

"Yes," Wade said.

Mason moved a little closer. "Tyler left the meeting first?"

"Yup."

"Jenkins left after him, right?"

"Yeah."

"You and Scott Bancroft had some words?"

"We did," Wade said. He looked at Mason with piercing eyes.

"You were angry with your partner for not going to his father, right?" Mason said, moving even closer to the witness box.

"You could say that."

"And you were angry with Jenkins for walking out?" Mason said, raising his voice.

"Yeah. That's right," Wade responded in kind.

Mason stood face-to-face with Wade. "You didn't work on equipment. You were putting tools away after tampering with the wiring?" Mason bellowed.

"That's a lie!"

"You left and saw Jenkins at a convenience store, right?"

Wade looked at Mason confused, like he was wondering how the lawyer could possibly know that. "No," Wade snapped.

Mason figured the pause in Wade's response meant that his instincts were correct. He'd noticed that the police report included a receipt form a gas station. Mason figured Wade had run into the old man there. And Wade probably wondered if he had security camera footage. The medical examiner's report postulated that Jenkins had been shot and brought to the mill, so Mason thought he was on the right track.

"You didn't see Jenkins at a convenience store?" Mason pressed.

"I might have seen him," Wade admitted. "But I didn't follow him there!"

"You followed him there," Mason hollered. "And you killed him with your .25 caliber pistol!"

"No, I didn't," Wade screamed. The tendons in his neck flexed like cables.

"You followed him. And you killed him. Because you're an angry man."

Mason turned away, intending to fetch a document from his table.

Wade stood up. "You bastard! You're tying to pin this all on me."

Then, he placed his hands on the edge of the witness box and leaped into the air, swinging his legs out of the box like a kid jumping a fence.

Wade landed on the floor and rushed at Mason.

The lawyer stepped aside and tripped Wade up, sticking a leg out. Mason drove the palm of his hand into Wade's back and drove the thug into the carpet.

Wade hit the deck and the wind was knocked out of him.

As Wade gasped for air, the bailiffs rushed over and pinned the man to the floor.

Mason cleared out of the way and headed over to the counsel

table.

When the dust settled, he found Tyler seated by Lexi trying to comfort her. She appeared shaken by the turn of events.

CHAPTER FORTY-FOUR

WEEKS after the Tyler Cummings trial ended, Mason headed down to his local coffee shop for an afternoon break.

The judge had declared a mistrial due to the incident with Wade.

Police had undertaken a routine inventory of Wade's belongings, including items found in his pickup truck after they arrested him for attacking Mason. They found Wade's pistol in the glovebox of the thug's pickup truck. Ballistics matched his gun to the one that had killed Jenkins. The finding led to a warrant and the police searched Wade's house. They found a deer rifle that matched ballistics from a round found at the mill the day Mason had been shot.

All this led to Cody Harper calling and dismissing the charges against Tyler with prejudice. Everything was pinned on Wade and the guy was going away for a very long time.

Entering the coffee shop, Mason walked across the repurposed hardwood flooring and ordered his usual black coffee. He didn't have anything pressing, so Mason found a seat by a window overlooking the Nashua River.

He watched the geese and seagulls frolicking in the water. Then, he pulled out his phone to check messages.

Mason went to take a sip of coffee when he noticed a familiar face at a nearby table.

Tyler Cummings was seated next to an attractive woman.

But the girl wasn't the same Lexi that Mason had met at court.

A moment later, the kid looked over and spotted Mason. Tyler smiled coolly.

Mason was confused by the situation. The two of them looked intimate.

Tyler walked over and asked if he could sit down.

"Sure," Mason said. "How can I help you?"

"Just wanted to thank you for everything," Tyler said. His voice sounded deeper, more confident.

"I was just doing my job." Mason looked at the girl. "That who I think it is?"

Tyler smiled. "Probably."

"Don't tell me," Mason said, putting things together. "Our investigator had picked up on the fact that Wade and Lexi had gone out of town together." Mason looked Tyler over. "Maybe you and Crystal figured out that your significant others were cheating, and so you set Wade up. You used Wade's pistol to kill Jenkins. Started the fire. Took a pot shot at me with one of Wade's rifles. Then made it easy for Wade to try and set you up with the gas can. It made you the perfect patsy."

"You said it counselor, not me," Tyler replied with a sardonic grin. Then the kid turned and walked away with an arrogant spring in his step.

ABOUT THE STORY

This story is a work of fiction and involves changes in physical locations and current criminal procedure in New Hampshire in order to make the book more cohesive. For instance, the courthouse located in Milford, New Hampshire is based upon a courthouse found in Laconia, New Hampshire. The Laconia courthouse is a refurbished schoolhouse, while the Milford courthouse is a fairly new structure.

New Hampshire has moved away from probable cause hearings in District Court, and so felonies are processed through grand juries. The District Courts are now referred to as Circuit Courts. The author hopes that these changes do not cause any distractions to readers.

ABOUT THE AUTHOR

John W. Dennehy is the author of the thrillers *Boston Law, Limited Damages, Arraigned,* and *Jurassic War*. After graduating from Pinkerton Academy, he enlisted in the U.S. Marines. He graduated from UNC Wilmington and Suffolk Law. John was a Litigation Partner at a Boston law firm for many years. He is a member of International Thriller Writers. He lives in New Hampshire, and can be found at his website: http://johnwdennehy.com/